AMARACHI'S TANGLED THREADS

FELIX SHABA (PhD)

Dedication

This book is dedicated to my beloved wife, Elizabeth Funmilayo Shaba. Your unwavering support, love, and encouragement have been my guiding light. Thank you for being my rock and my inspiration.

Chapter One:
Horizon

The 3rd of August was a day Amarachi would never forget. She had just returned from fetching water in the stream for her grandmother to bathe that afternoon, and she decided to soak garri with coconut for lunch. Just as she was about to pour the garri into a rubber cup, a familiar voice, like the sudden gust of wind in a still forest, sliced through her tranquilly and pierced through the compound.

"Amarachi! Amarachi!" Ifeoma's voice echoed as she rushed through the gate, her desperation cutting through the stillness of the afternoon. Amarachi wondered why Ifeoma would be screaming her name in such a thunderous manner. Her heart pounded as she watched Ifeoma make her way into the room with bated breath.

Amarachi placed the jug of water in her hand on the table as Ifeoma entered her room.

"So, you are here, and I have been shouting your name, but you did not answer me?" Ifeoma complained.

"Of course, I'm here," Amarachi replied casually. *"I'm just about to soak garri for the afternoon."*

"Soak gini?" Ifeoma inquired, her voice rising in surprise.

"Why would you even think of soaking garri today of all days? "Have you forgotten that the entire village and neighbourhood have already gathered in the market square for the Nkaonu festival? She

continued, her words laden with urgency.

"Oh, that is true, but I really don't feel like going anywhere, Ifeoma," Amarachi said nonchalantly. "Are you kidding me?" Ifeoma angrily removed the garri and water jug from the table and placed them in one corner of the room.

"Who will believe that we are the only ones who didn't witness the Nkaonu festival?" She exclaimed.

The gentle rays of the noon sun illuminated the room, adding a comforting atmosphere to Amarachi's daily life. The torn curtains fluttered softly, creating light and shadow patterns that accentuated the simplicity of the room. The walls, adorned by fading Osadebe posters and vibrant fabrics, held tales of shared moments. As the window let in snippets of the festival's music and giggling from the festival, Amarachi found herself drawn to Ifeoma's urgency. A shaky wooden table filled with well-worn textbooks and an old hurricane light, bearing witness to the midnight study rites, stood at the heart of the room.

"Is there something significant happening at the festival?" She inquired, realizing Ifeoma's determination to attend.

"What in the world are you talking about?" Ifeoma echoed incredulously.

"Do you want to tell me that you don't know what the Nkaonu festival is all about?" She exclaimed, her eyes reflecting both enthusiasm and disappointment.

"Besides the dynamic and unique nature of the festival, this year promises something different, judging from the many days of announcements, which you yourself are well aware of. It is a year of general homecoming."

Amarachi found herself at a loss for words, realizing she could do nothing to persuade Ifeoma. She rose from the edge of the spring bed and dressed, leaving behind the garri. Ifeoma dragged her out of the room, and both went straight towards the lively market square.

As Amarachi rushed alongside Ifeoma towards the market square, the beat of the drums grew stronger, enveloping the atmosphere with electrifying energy that sparked a thrilling blend of anticipation and curiosity within her.

"Mmamma." Both of them greeted the elders in unison as they passed through the busy footpath.

"Mmamma, good and beautiful children." They responded, trudging along.

The festival was alive with energy. A colourful mix of people dressed in traditional attire danced and celebrated the Nkaonu festival with pure joy.

Amidst the lively crowd, Amarachi's mind flickered with memories of her past glory when she was the lead dancer and a star among her peers at the tender ages of fifteen and sixteen. The echoes of applause still rang in her ears, leaving her humbled and unable to walk the streets without being stopped for days. Now seventeen, she had made the difficult decision to step away from the limelight, focusing instead on her studies for the forthcoming WAEC and NECO exams. Yet, as she stood amidst the pulsating energy of the festival, she found herself irresistibly drawn to its vibrancy. The stark contrast between the festival's liveliness and the tranquillity of her grandmother's home struck her with poignant intensity. Positioning herself alongside Ifeoma at a strategic vantage point, they yielded to the captivating spectacle unfolding before them. Engulfed by the mixture of events, they became oblivious to the passage of time.

The Nkaonu Festival has transformed the once bustling market square into a canvas of cultural richness, with each moment unfolding like a masterpiece awaiting discovery.

As the buzzing rhythm of drums reverberated through the bustling market square, a group of enthusiastic young men confidently made their way towards Amarachi and Ifeoma.

"Who's that girl over there?" Mr Linus asked, staring in fascination and fixing his eyes on a figure in the distance. He was momentarily dumbstruck by the girl's radiant smile.

"Which of them? There are so many girls over there, you know," replied his friend, casting a curious glance in the same direction.

"There's one standing on the mound close to the Achi tree, and there's another girl standing beside her." He pointed, revealing delicate-looking fingers that had not seen farm work for years.

"Follow my finger."

His friend followed his gaze, scanning the crowd before nodding in recognition.

"Oh! The village beauty?" He flashed a sly look at his friend and added, *"That's the village beauty."*

"Really?" Mr Linus nodded eagerly; his curiosity piqued. *"I'd like to get acquainted with her."*

"With who? Hia! That girl is very reserved; what awaits you is disappointment," his friend warned, shaking his head.

His friend hesitated, offering a word of caution.

"But there is no harm in trying." Mr Linus insisted with

determination in his voice.

"I won't stop you. But don't say I didn't warn you about a trial that will amount to nothing," his friend cautioned, a hint of concern in his tone.

"You haven't seen the world yet." Mr Linus boasted, and the two friends again exchanged glances.

Amidst the boisterous celebration with fireworks going off everywhere and the heavy sound of cannons and Dane guns complimenting them from time to time, the dancers in the arena went into a frenzy of different displays of muscles and twisting of various body parts so that the spectators went wild with thunderous cheers and applause.

For Amarachi, the spectacle was more than just entertainment; it was a journey into a world of hidden knowledge and wisdom. As she watched the dancers, memories of her own training flooded her mind, intertwining with the scenes unfolding before her. At that moment, she realised that, amidst the chaos of the festival, she was being guided towards a deeper understanding of herself and her heritage.

First, men who were probably in their fifties were advancing slowly and majestically to the arena, heralded by the instrumentalists, who stood briefly in the centre before settling down to sit astride their instruments or on makeshift stools. They expertly performed all this without disrupting the rhythm of the music. When they fully entered the arena, their attire was on full display. Each man wore a brilliant red George-style cloth around his waist, flowing down to his ankles, while a chieftaincy Isiagu adorned his top, complete with a marching red cap. They swayed gently at the beginning to the beating of the drums as they formed a circle around the instrumentalists. With the *oji* in their hands, they pierced the earth as they moved.

Then, the man with the ója, also colourfully dressed, with an eagle's feather stuck to his cap, began to release a variety of notes that blended well with the rest of the instruments. However, his entrance changed the tempo of the music; in that very instance, all the oji in the hands of the men flew out and stood together in a bunch close to the instrumentalists, signifying unity. It was then that the fans hanging on the men's wrists came into view. They held them aloft for a while until they became a magnificent canopy of multiple materials and colours; some were made of feathers, and others were of a mixture of straw and fabrics of different sorts. Again, in one quick move, the fans sailed smoothly, plummeted as a starry circle, and then covered the centre like a royal carpet.

Without warning to the spectators, who were already wild with excitement over the men's performance, a single jingle of the bell was heard, and the men immediately began to vibrate their shoulders and chest muscles with astonishing speed, still in response to the rhythm of the instrumentalists. The Ja man stood rigidly tall in a spot, coordinating the entire proceedings with his melodious tunes.

Amarachi's understanding was like a voice expounding things to her at each step of the proceedings in the arena.

"True progress comes where there is unity and the appropriate use of authority, and when this happens, peace becomes a natural outcome." Her smile broadened further upon this illumination. She reasoned that the fans represented wealth, and the dancers simply demonstrated the comfort and honour they provided when properly managed. The men's shoulders and chests vibrated, indicating creativity, diligence, and hard work, without which the two in the centre, the *oji* and the fan, would not exist.

When the men completed their session, they narrowed the circle without breaking up. Still dancing, they stood around the royal carpet, picking up the fans and hanging them back on. Each man pulled up his *oji*. This time, with the òja man in the lead, the men retreated in the same way they came into the arena.

As the men exited, a group of middle-aged, gorgeously dressed women entered the arena. They were not in any way inferior to the men; they exuded bravery, strength, and joy as they stepped gracefully into the dancing area. Their headgear was so exquisitely made that it looked more like crowns on them. Each woman was richly decked with ivory and coral beads, which blended perfectly with the shimmering short-sleeved blouse she had on, and she tied a double-piece red background with multiple colours around her waist that reached down to the ankle.

They sang and danced together with their instrumentalists, who were also women, waving the horses' tails in their right hands in the air. At this point, every part of their body was involved in the dance as they circled around and around. Suddenly, the instrumentalists moved to the centre, swiftly closing the gap in the circle. Just then, a thrilling burst of melody ripped through the air; the singing stopped, and the women's waists began to vibrate with astonishing speed, moving gingerly forward in formation.

Amarachi was highly fascinated. *"How can they multitask in this manner?"* she gasped. However, as she looked on, particularly at the instrumentalists whose waists were also vibrating, her brain lubricated, *"Indeed, women multitask! Mothers, housekeepers, carers, workers, wives, business managers, and indeed, the belt that binds them all together are examples of how women multitask. Could that be the connection to the horses' tails in their hands? This is it! These are symbols of strength and resilience; anything that negatively affects the core that bears the burden leads to a total collapse of the whole unit."*

She was so lost in her cogitations that she did not realise when the women retreated and were quickly replaced by young, vibrant girls about her age. She was only brought back to the present by the cries of excitement that followed the former and ushered in the youngsters.

She had been a part of them more than once, so she did not have any difficulties understanding the lessons about their style of dancing. It simply pointed to the future they represented: hopes, dreams, and procreation were all incubated into reality by the strength of this portion of the body. However, she watched them with sincere admiration, not blinking once. The brightly coloured blouses they wore stopped a little above the navel, exposing the *jigida* around their waists. Then, their skirts flowed decorously below their knees. Each ankle bore a string of *ekpiri* around it that produced distinct sounds that synchronized perfectly with the music. Like the women, they were their own instrumentalists, and they took turns performing that function.

They danced in groups of eight damsels at a time, wearing disarming smiles on their faces, and young men began to hallucinate. The girls danced so vigorously and well that the crowd started showering them with money. They concentrated their own vibrations on the stomach, which explains why they were exposed. From time to time, the girls looked in a particular direction, which aroused curiosity in some of the spectators who observed it.

Amarachi unwittingly vibrated her stomach in harmony with the dancers in the arena, moving her hands and legs in such a dignified manner that she seemed to be coordinating the activities from her position. It was more like a dancing queen receiving homage from her subordinates.

Ifeoma was taken aback when she observed what was happening, but it was too late for her to do anything; she could only stand and watch helplessly. She noticed how the girl playing the stringed instrument looked fixedly at Amarachi, whose movement seemed to determine the tunes she released. However, Amarachi, who by this time knew they looked up to her, did not disappoint; she fully connected with them and displayed a variety of dancing steps that even Ifeoma had never seen. When it was time for them to retreat, she gave them a signal with the jerking of her eyebrow and a smile, which they all returned as they exited the arena amidst a tumultuous shout.

Then, a long clanging of the *ogele* resounded, and the entire market square fell into dead silence. It was the high point of the occasion when the history of the village was re-enacted and made alive through the performances and dramatisation of unique events in the land. The times of difficulties and troubles were represented by the slow motions and appearances of bizarre masquerades, and Amarachi was poised to get as many details as she could on this occasion.

"Excuse me, ladies, may I have the pleasure of joining your delightful gathering?" Mr Linus inquired in an attempt to strike up a conversation.

Amarachi and Ifeoma shared a mischievous look upon noticing his shining bald head, recognising the interruption, before calmly stating, *"Our presence here is solely to observe the enchanting proceedings in the arena, not to be entertained by any diversions.*

Unfazed by Amarachi's dismissive attitude, the young men eagerly continued to initiate conversations with the two friends.

"Come on, don't be so serious. We are just here to have a great time at the festival," another young man added with a charming smile.

Ifeoma, the ever-outgoing of the two, responded with a warm smile and tried to lighten the mood with a playful comment. *"Oh, how interesting to see you here. Unfamiliar presence among yearly admirers. Of course, feel free to join the club,"* she proposed, casting a mischievous glance at Amarachi in order to draw her attention to the young man's appearance. He was so dark that he appeared to be painted with charcoal. But surprisingly, he had the advantage of red lips that formed a beautiful frame around his flashing, perfect set of teeth whenever he smiled.

Amarachi, though firm in her determination, kept her eyes locked on the mesmerising dance of the masquerades, but not without noticing Ifeoma's hint. *"I would rather fully enjoy the festival without any unnecessary interruptions,"* she restated in a resolute yet courteous tone.

Amarachi's unwavering attention to the events captivated Mr. Linus. He marvelled at her resolute and steadfast dedication to fully embrace her quest like an explorer, even in the midst of a chaotic market square. He approached Amarachi and Ifeoma with a mixture of admiration and curiosity, his demeanour displaying respect and a hint of intrigue. *"Your keen interest in the festival's cultural traditions is quite evident,"* he commented, his voice brimming with warmth and hospitality.

"Certainly, the Nkaonu festival is momentous for us," Ifeoma confessed.

As Mr. Linus and his friends positioned themselves in front of the two ladies, hoping to capture their attention, Amarachi remained unfazed, though she found them a little disgusting. With unwavering concentration, she leaned forward, and her gaze locked onto the feverish performance that was reaching its peak as the drumming reached a crescendo in front of her. The young men exchanged puzzled glances, utterly perplexed by the sheer captivation displayed by the individual in front of them.

Ifeoma, who suddenly found interest in the man, was not happy with Amarachi's snobbish attitude, and she did not hide this even in the presence of the visitors.

"Let me tell you, Amarachi, the Nkaonu festival is about so much more than just masquerades. It's a time when one must skilfully navigate through a sea of persistent suitors," Ifeoma remarked. As the young men stood somewhat flustered, Ifeoma continued, *"In Amufigbo and its environs, Nkaonu's festival is akin to a grand networking event. While some individuals seek cultural experience, others view it as a chance to forge unique connections."*

Amarachi responded with an indifferent shrug while still trying to figure out the meaning of the patterns made by the masquerade on the floor of the arena. *"Well, I'm here for the cultural experience, not to entertain any suitors or forge connections,"* she remarked casually, her tone indicating her disinterest in the social aspect of the festival.

Regardless of Ifeoma's efforts to engage her in discussions about suitors and connections, Amarachi remained captivated by the enchanting performances that unfolded before her.

"I must say, I've never experienced anything quite like this. I live in London but came from the Umunaka village to witness the festivities." Mr Linus explained.

Undeterred by Amarachi's reserved demeanour, he continued, *"I couldn't help but notice how you both seem to be in a world of your own, especially you, Amarachi."*

Amarachi, sensing the direction of the conversation, replied curtly, *"Well, we're here for the festival, not small talk."*

11

Ifeoma, catching on to the tension, intervened with a light-hearted tone: *"Come on, Amarachi, Mr London, here is just trying to be sociable." No harm in that, right?"*

Amarachi, however, remained unyielding, her gaze fixed back on the masquerades. *"I prefer to enjoy the festival in peace."*

Mr Linus, slightly stunned, attempted to salvage the conversation. *"I didn't mean to intrude. I just thought it's always nice to make new friends, especially during such vibrant celebrations."*

However, Amarachi did not sway. *"I appreciate the sentiment, but I'd rather enjoy the festival on my own. Excuse me."*

With that, Amarachi gracefully excused herself, leaving the three strangers and Ifeoma in an awkward silence. Ifeoma, trying to diffuse the tension, said, *'Do not mind her; she's always been like that during the festival. She takes the masquerades very seriously."*

Mr Linus, still somewhat puzzled, replied, *"I see. Well, it was a pleasure to meet you both. I'll let you get back to your festival."*

As Mr Linus walked away, Ifeoma could not help but chuckle. *"You really know how to put up a wall, Amarachi."*

Amarachi, unfazed, replied, *"I just want to enjoy the festival without unnecessary distractions. Let's get back to the masquerades."*

Once again, the two friends immersed themselves in the enchanting world of the Nkaonu festival, leaving Mr Linus and his two friends to navigate the lively crowd on their own.

Immersed in the vibrant atmosphere of the masquerades, Mr Linus found himself overcome by introspection, still grappling with the lingering sting of Amarachi's rejection. With every stride he made amidst the bustling crowd, a symphony of unanswered questions echoed in the air.

"What is it about her?" The mysterious charm of Amarachi's enigmatic presence intrigued and perplexed him as he pondered. The way she carried herself as if guarding a multitude of hidden truths, or the defiance in her gaze that resists forming bonds.

"Not even the mention of London could sway her; rather, it felt more like encountering an insurmountable barrier as she remained guarded within her self-imposed walls. "Is Amarachi an enigma waiting to be unravelled or a conundrum with no answer?"

As Ifeoma watched Mr Linus depart amidst the vibrant festival ambience, a fleeting sense of letdown crossed her typically jovial countenance. She experienced a gentle stir of unexpressed longing for connection. As the masquerades continued their lively dancing, her mind drifted into a delightful daydream.

"What if he had paid me more attention?" She contemplated allowing her creativity to explore endless possibilities. *"We could have exchanged tales about London, a city that has always been a figment of my imagination. Immersed in the charm of its streets and captivated by its vibrant events, perhaps he held the potential to bring those dreams to life."* Amidst the captivating allure of the festival, the boundaries of reality appeared flexible, leaving one to ponder the realm of possibilities.

Meanwhile, Amarachi found herself caught between irritation and amusement as she observed Mr Linus' feeble attempts amid the pulsating rhythm of the masquerades. Despite Mr London's presence, her determination remained unwavering, adding a hint of drama to the spectacle.

"London or not, it makes no difference," she pondered, her eyes locked on the captivating performance unfolding before her. *"I am not influenced by individuals who use their background as a weapon of manipulation and control. His futile efforts only strengthened my resolve to enjoy the festival without interruption fully. No extravagant backstory can penetrate the stronghold of my solitude."*

Amarachi, confidently taking the lead, could not help but perceive the subtle currents of emotions flowing through her friend. While Ifeoma was lost in thought, Amarachi interrupted the silence with a casual inquiry: *"Are you enjoying the festival, Ifeoma?"*

Caught off-guard, Ifeoma's heart skipped a beat. *"Oh, you know me, Amarachi! "I love the festival vibes, dances, and masquerades. It's so invigorating!"* She responded with forced enthusiasm, desperately trying to conceal the subtle disappointment lingering within.

Amarachi raised her eyebrows, perceiving a deeper layer of information. Nevertheless, to respect Ifeoma's privacy, she refrained from probing further. Unknown to her, within the festival's echoes, each person harboured a distinct melody in his or her heart, and the night held the potential for countless stories and unexpected twists.

As Mr Linus left the festival grounds with his friends, curiosity lingered in the air, like whispers. His friends, eager to learn more about his impression, couldn't help but inquire about his interactions with Amarachi and Ifeoma.

"So, spill it, Linus. How did it go with those two lovely ladies?" One of his friends, Ikechukwu, who had tried helping out and teased him with a mischievous glint in his eye.

Mr Linus, still wrapped in contemplation of Amarachi's mystery, offered a subdued smile.

"Well, let's just say Amarachi isn't the easiest person to converse with. Ifeoma was more open but decided not to join us."

His friends exchanged glances and understood the dynamics of Amarachi's personality within the community.

"Amarachi has a reputation for being reserved in the village," Uba, the other of his friends who said nothing during their encounter with Amarachi, commented. *"In fact, that aspect of her, beyond her enchanting beauty, is actually what draws all kinds of men to her. However, just as termites in a nuptial flight often find themselves knocked down, captured, or killed due to their flocking around a fire, the same fate has befallen many men emotionally and socially."* He licked his dry, thick lips and continued, *"You know the urge to conquer can be intoxicating and destroy clear judgment. That girl only turned seventeen this year. You won't believe it unless someone tells you."* He rolled his large eyes like a child, trying to recall something. *"At twelve, that girl was already taller than many eighteen-year-olds with everything full. You know what I mean. The only trace of her real age is her ever-so-cheerful babyface. Even now, is she not like mammy water with no flaws at all?"*

"The shocking part about that girl I find fascinating is her strength." Ikechukwu chimed in, *"If you think you're a man, go and try her on a good day on the farm. While you're still struggling with one portion, she's gone through ten portions. The day I observed this, I stood rooted to the ground for a long time, wondering whether my eyes were playing tricks on me."*

The trio decided to continue the night at a nearby palm wine joint. As they settled into the rustic ambience, Mr Linus, feeling a blend of frustration and fascination, ordered a keg of palm wine and three servings of chevon pepper soup.

Throughout their lively banter and laughter, Amarachi's image persisted in Linus' thoughts. The yellow gown that reached down below her knees seemed customized for her alone. Her near-pink complexion was not like anything he had seen before. He could still see her sharp, penetrating brown eyes, which could disarm any man. Her defiant, pointed nose stood her out among many, giving her a queenly aura. It was not just her beauty or youthfulness that captivated him; there was an elusive quality and a mysterious allure that lingered in his mind.

"I can't get her out of my head," Mr Linus confessed to his friends when the conversation veered towards other topics. *"There's something about Amarachi that's more than meets the eye. I can't quite put my finger on it."*

"Are you already taken?" He asked his friends about nudism and exchanged amused glances, teasing him about being smitten by the enigmatic village beauty.

Despite jesting, Mr Linus could not shake the sense that Amarachi held significance beyond its surface allure.

The night wore on; palm wine flowed, and laughter echoed through the dimly lit joint.

As the night came to a close, Mr Linus, who was still preoccupied with Amarachi's thoughts, made an unexpected proposal.

With a determined tone, he asked, *"Do any of you know where Amarachi lives?"*

His friends looked at each other with intrigue as the abrupt question took them aback. Mr Linus' unusually urgent statement regarding the villager was surprising.

"What is your motive for inquiring about her house?" Ikechukwu questioned him, displaying a perplexed expression and furrowed

eyebrows.

After much thought, Mr Linus finally said, *"I need to speak with her about something important."*

His friends seemed to be at the edge of their seats, wondering what Mr Linus' request meant.

"We warned you before, and you wouldn't listen. What do you really want?" Ikechukwu reminded everyone after a brief moment of silence, and everyone fell into deep silence again.

"Her house is located nearby, a short distance from the Catholic Primary School, next to the Ukwa tree," Uba remarked, interrupting the period of silence that had enveloped them.

Mr Linus thanked his friends, paid the bills, and bid them goodnight.

As they parted ways, his friends could not shake off the intrigue that lingered in the air. *"What do you think he wants with Amarachi?"* one of them whispered, asking a question that weighed both of their thoughts.

As darkness enveloped the village, Amarachi hesitated at the outer edges of the bustling square, her steps heavy and reluctant. The Nkaonu Festival's bustling energy remained in the atmosphere, resonating with the rhythm of her investigative heart.

Ifeoma, her unwavering companion, remained by her side and served as a gentle symbol of the strong connection that bound them. *"Amarachi, it is time for us to return home,"* she implored, her voice gently beseeching amidst the lively atmosphere.

Amarachi paused, her gaze fixed on the glittering lights swaying in the distance. *"I had no initial desire to be here in the first place;*

you dragged me here, so why are you in a hurry to go home?" she asked.

Ifeoma's serene smile radiated understanding as she remarked, *"It's quite unusual how you embraced the festival more than myself, the one who brought you here."* Her words carried a playful tease, accompanied by a mischievous glint in her eyes. *"But now, it's time we made our way back home."*

At that moment, Amarachi realised that she had not eaten lunch!

They weaved through the throngs of festivalgoers side by side, and their laughter harmonised with the evening music.

"Why did you not give Mr Linus an audience?" Ifeoma remarked sarcastically that they distanced themselves from lively tunes.

"Audience?" Amarachi replied, and her irritation was evident. *"What did you expect me to do?"* she retorted.

Ifeoma glanced sideways in Amarachi's direction, a known expression of her features.

"You know, Amarachi, it's pretty obvious that Mr Linus is interested in you," she remarked, her tone tinged with playful mischief.

Amarachi shrugged nonchalantly. *"Is he? I did not notice,"* she replied, and her voice was devoid of any hints of interest.

"But didn't you see the way he kept trying to engage you in conversation?" Ifeoma persisted, her curiosity piqued.

Amarachi waved off the notion with a dismissive gesture. *"He's just being polite,"* Ifeoma said. *It's nothing."* She replied; her indifference was palpable.

As they went in separate directions, Ifeoma found herself consumed by Mr Linus' thoughts and could not shake the feeling that there was more to Mr Linus' interest in Amarachi than mere politeness. The mystery of his seemingly indifferent attitude towards her lingered in her mind, creating a whirlwind of curiosity and anticipation. She was so engrossed in her musings that she nearly breezed past the gate of her own house.

Amarachi's grandmother was in the kitchen preparing Akpu when she entered the house. Ngozi's eyes sparkled with anticipation as she assisted her grandmother, and her curiosity was piqued by the stories she knew Amarachi would soon share. Despite having the opportunity to join the festivities, Ngozi's commitment to family duties led her to the fields earlier in the day to collect firewood. Rather than rush off to partake in the excitement, she stayed back to help Grandma with house chores.

"Dalu grandma." Amarachi greeted the old woman as she collected the pestle from her to pound the akpu.

"My daughter, how are you?" She responded. *"How did the festival go?"* She asked with a beaming smile.

"Nne nkeukwu, the festival went well." Amarachi replied.

As the pestle rhythmically pounded against the akpu mortar, Ngozi could not contain her excitement.

"Tell me everything, Amarachi!" How was the festival?" She chirped eagerly as she awaited her elder sister to give her the full gist; her eyes gleamed with anticipation.

Amarachi grinned; her voice dropped almost to whispering as she recounted the vibrant scenes from the Nkaonu Festival.

"Oh, Ngozi, you wouldn't believe it! I discovered a whole lot of

new things today, and the masquerades were like nothing I had seen before. They danced as if the whole village was their stage!" she exclaimed.

As the sisters retired to their room, the day's events still lingered in their thoughts, weaving a tapestry of memories that begged them to be revisited.

Ngozi's eyes sparkled with interest. *"Tell me more. Did you meet anyone interesting there?"*

"Oh yeah, there was this man called Mr Linus that came to interrupt our peace with his two friends; he said that he came from London."

Ngozi burst into laughter, and the sound echoed through their bedroom. "A London man in our village! Imagine that! What was he looking for?"

"Oh, because he's from London, he must be expecting a red-carpet welcome, right? Like, wow, London, big deal!" Amarachi scoffed and dramatically rolled her eyes. "I bet he thought I'd be all, 'Oh, Mr London Man, please grace us with your presence!' However, I treated him with the iciest attitude he had ever seen. London, my foot! Give me a break, biko!"

Ngozi giggled, imagining the scene. "I can just picture it! "Amarachi, the unbothered queen, ignoring the London man and his entourage,' she teased.

Amarachi laughed along with the joyous camaraderie she shared with her sister. As they shared the festival tales and laughed at Mr Linus' antics, Amarachi felt grateful for their bond.

The two ladies snuggled under their blankets, and in just a few minutes, Amarachi dozed off.

Before the sudden death of their mother, Ijeoma, Amarachi and Ngozi lived with their parents very close to their grandmother's house. Mr Ejiofo, their father, felt immense pressure due to a lack of a male heir, as the expectations of his kinsmen tested his patience. Ijeoma watched her husband's battle with a heavy heart, feeling weighed down by their circumstances and overshadowed by the disappointment hanging over their family.

One evening, under the heavy burden of their hopes, Ijeoma confidently approached her husband.

"My love, listen to me," she started, her voice gentle but determined. *"I understand the expectations from your family, but I am confident that we will have a son when the time is right." Our two daughters are precious to us, and they are our bundles of joy. We should not allow the pressure from your kinsmen to make us feel as if girls are not children.".*

With unwavering conviction, her words resonated through the stillness of their home, providing a glimmer of hope amid uncertainty.

The birth of their third daughter, though initially greeted with hopeful anticipation, soon gave way to bitter disappointment. The kinsmen, clad in the armour of tradition, found the situation a good weapon to scatter the peaceful home they were quite jealous of. They minced no words as they voiced their disapproval in the very halls of the maternity home. Their disdain cut through the air like a sharpened blade, leaving Ijeoma and Mr Ejiofor reeling from the sting of their callous words.

Barely twenty-one days after Ogochi was born, Mr Ejiofor, wearied and exasperated, found himself entangled in a heated argument with his relentless kinsmen.

"Another girl?" One of the kinsmen sneered, his tone dripping with contempt.

"You've failed us yet again, Ejiofor. You must produce a male heir, Ejiofor! Our lineage depends on it," another kinsman bellowed, his voice echoing through the air like a thunderclap.

"I've done everything in my power. Fate has given me daughters," Mr Ejiofor retorted, a mix of frustration and helplessness etched across his face.

Ijeoma and Mr Ejiofor were devastated when Ogochi, who was barely three months old, suddenly cried out of her sleep one afternoon, her tiny body burning with fever. Despite their best efforts, Ogochi's health declined rapidly, leading to her passing and leaving an irreplaceable void. The couple wept uncontrollably, their sorrow consuming them.

Yet their relatives displayed no compassion. Two of their relatives showed a lack of empathy by celebrating Ogochi's death, commenting that it had decreased the number of *"female burdens"* in the family. Their cruel words pierced deeply, intensifying Ijeoma and Mr Ejiofor's pain.

As time passed, the pressure from their relatives grew stronger. It loomed ominously above them, a persistent symbol of their family's perceived flaws. Ijeoma found it difficult to find peace amid turmoil, her previously lively demeanour overshadowed by hopelessness.

Another unfortunate event occurred just one month later, adding to Mr Ejiofor's already existing pain. Ijeoma, weighed down by the expectations of her husband's kinsmen, became seriously ill. The clash between Mr Ejiofor and their relatives further intensified Ijeoma's distress. She listened intently, a mix of anger and sadness washing over her as she realised the impact of the constant pressure on her husband.

Ijeoma's sudden illness cast a shadow over their once-vibrant home as the cruel hands of fate tightened their grip. Despite their desperate efforts, Ijeoma's condition worsened with each passing day until one fateful night when she summoned her eldest daughter, Amarachi, to her bedside.

"You are my strength, my precious daughter. No matter what happens, stand tall and face life with courage," Ijeoma imparted, her voice a soft murmur that lingered in Amarachi's heart. The next morning, Ijeoma's spirit departed, leaving behind a grieving husband and two young daughters, their world shattered by loss.

In the wake of Ijeoma's passing, Mr Ejiofor found himself torn between grief and the harsh realities of their circumstances. Barely six months had passed since his beloved wife's departure, yet the kinsmen wasted no time in renewing their relentless demands for a male heir.

"You must have another wife, Ejiofor." The lineage must continue," they insisted, their voices unyielding. With a heavy heart and a sense of duty weighing heavily upon his shoulders, Mr Ejiofor succumbed to their pressure, seeking solace in the arms of another woman they recommended.

As the new wife, Nkechi, entered their lives, Amarachi and her little sister found themselves thrust into a world fraught with uncertainty and upheaval. Nkechi's arrival brought with it a tide of resentment and hostility, her disdain for her stepdaughters evident in every word and deed.

One evening, tensions reached a boiling point, and confrontation filled the air. Nkechi's bitter words pierced the silence, assaulting Amarachi and her sister's fragile hearts.

"You are both good for nothing, and that is why your mother was unable to bear your father a son before she died of her witchcraft." Nkechi spat, her words a venomous assault on their fragile hearts.

Amarachi, fuelled by her newfound resolve, stood her ground. *"We are not responsible for the circumstances surrounding our birth."* Our mother loved us, and that love will forever be a part of us," she declared, her gaze unwavering.

In the face of Nkechi's hostility, the two sisters could no longer bear the beating and incessant starving, not to mention the idea of sending them to fetch water from the stream at odd hours. As Nkechi raised her hand to hit Amarachi, she was shocked when Amarachi's left hand shot out like iron pliers, held the hand mid-air, and looked defiantly into her eyes.

"Don't you ever dare?" Her eyes were sharp and piercing like knives, stabbing straight into Nkechi's heart. *"I love and respect my father. If not, he-he!"*

The woman was dazed; however, she ignored the warning and felt she could intimidate Amarachi by throwing a punch at her, but her hand was thrown backwards with a rocklike blow that sent her brain reeling. Before she could regain consciousness, Amarachi and her sister packed the little things they could lay their hands on and sought refuge in their paternal grandmother's home. The old woman, a pillar of strength who had heard of the ill-treatment beacon placed on them by the new wife, welcomed them with open arms.

It was in this compound that Amarachi found the stability and support she needed to complete her secondary education. As she awaited the release of her WAEC and NECO results, Amarachi navigated the delicate balance between her dreams and the harsh realities of her past. Her grandmother's house, though not adorned with grandeur, became a haven of hope and resilience in the face of adversity. The threads of her life, intricately woven with trials and triumphs, held the promise of a future waiting to be untangled.

Chapter Two:
Amarachi Gets Married

The day after the Nkaonu Festival, Amarachi was too tired to get up from bed. She would have loved to sleep a little longer, but when she realized there was no water in the house for their grandmother to bathe with, she quickly picked up the bucket and headed to the stream. She had barely entered her room after fetching the water when the grandmother called her.

"Oo nne! I'm coming." She promptly answered but then muttered, *"What could Ne be calling me for now?"*

"Oge was here to ask after you when you went to fetch water for me from the stream." The old woman stated.

Amarachi scowled at the news, muttering to herself, *"Why would that brat be looking for me?"* Memories of the day at the stream flashed through her mind when she had to assert herself against Oge's rudeness. The two had not been on speaking terms since then, and Amarachi could not fathom what could cause Oge to come seeking her now.

Bewildered by the unexpected visit, Amarachi hesitated as she approached the gate. As she reluctantly stepped out, her eyes widened at the sight of Mr Linus and his friends, who stood by the coconut tree that demarcated their compound and Oge's.

Amarachi's initial instinct was to retreat, but before she could make a move, Mr Linus rushed forward, extending a hand as if to bridge the gap between them. *"Amarachi, please, just listen to what*

I have to say," he pleaded.

Amarachi, with her guard still firmly in place, arched an eyebrow. *"What's this all about?"*

Mr Linus, with a gentle smile, replied, *"We just want to talk, share stories, and get to know each other."*

As Amarachi remained sceptical, Ikechukwu and Uba stepped forward to provide him succour, recognising her from previous encounters in the village.

"Hey, Amarachi, I am sure you know us very well in this village," Ikechukwu said, extending a hand.

Amarachi, although wary, nodded. *"Yes, I know you both, but what's this talk all about?"*

Uba chimed in, *"We're just here for a friendly chat; no harm is intended." "Mr Linus speaks highly of you."*

Amarachi, now caught between curiosity and caution, softened her stance. *"Highly of me? Why?"*

"Because you're an intriguing person, Amarachi." Mr Linus stepped in, unwilling to lose the opportunity. *"My friends shared a bit about you, and I wanted to hear more from you directly."*

For the first time, she relaxed her defences and lowered the walls she had built around her heart for many years to embrace the possibility of connection and investigate the reality of their claim. To guard against her grandmother's wrath, Amarachi suggested they walk down the street towards the primary school.

As the conversation unfolded, Amarachi found herself slowly warming up to the trio. The friends, recognising her initial reservations, shared stories of their own, creating an atmosphere of companionship.

"I've never had friends from outside the village before," Amarachi admitted, a genuine smile playing on her lips.

As they walked down the street, Mr Linus, seizing the opportunity, replied, *"Well, sometimes the best connections come from unexpected places.".*

The walk transformed into a mix of laughter, cultural sharing, and deeper comprehension. Mr Linus' friends acted as a bridge, easing the initial doubts and uncertainties.

As Mr. Linus and his friends journeyed back to their village, the night air resonated with the anticipation of fresh beginnings, leaving Amarachi with a profound feeling of connection and potential that transcended the confines of their individual worlds.

The sun dipped low on the horizon, casting a warm glow over the village as Amarachi made her way back home, oblivious to the impending tide of change.

The matriarch's wise gaze locked with Amarachi's upon her arrival at the compound. "Amarachi, I observed you strolling with unfamiliar faces down the street," she remarked, her tone cautious. *"Be careful; not everyone has good intentions. Do you recall the near-kidnapping of Chinyere saved by the eagle eyes of the vigilante groups?"*

Amarachi nodded, taking in her grandmother's counsel. *"Grandma, I understand. But these 'strangers' were actually Mr. Linus and his two friends from our own village."*

Her grandmother, though satisfied with the explanation, maintained a cautious demeanour. *"In our world, everyone is a stranger until proven otherwise."*

The following morning, Amarachi felt a sense of urgency to share her latest experience with Ifeoma. To avoid a backlog of duties, she hurriedly swept the compound twice as fast as usual and wrapped up her other morning chores, knowing it would be a long talk. She made her way to Ifeoma's house with determined, long strides, the morning sun creating a gentle light on the village paths.

As Amarachi stepped into Ifeoma's humble abode, she saw her gazing out the window, deep in contemplation. Her face was still swollen with unfinished sleep. In the calm of the morning, Amarachi sat down next to her and got ready to recount the events of the previous evening.

"Ifeoma, did you stay up late last night?" Amarachi enquired.

"How did you find out?" she asked.

"It's written all over your face. And you look somewhat pale," Amarachi said.

"I actually didn't sleep on time. I don't know what kept me awake," Ifeoma confirmed.

"How did you cope with the calls of nocturnal creatures?" Amarachi teased.

"At my age?" "I don't fear those things anymore." Ifeoma shrugged, wiping her fleshy, yellow face with the tip of her wrapper.

"It's like that sometimes anyway. Only God can explain reasons for certain things." She fidgeted with her fingers for a while and fell silent. Ifeoma observed her agitation but decided not to pressure her, so she pretended not to notice.

"Ifeoma," Amarachi began, her voice gentle yet resolute, *"I need to tell you about what happened last night."*

Ifeoma turned towards her, her eyes reflecting a mixture of curiosity and worry. *"What's happening, Amarachi? You seem troubled."*

Amarachi took a deep breath and began narrating her story about Mr Linus and his unexpected visit, along with the surprising events that unfolded. Her words lingered in the air; the weight of the moment was palpable between them as she spoke.

As Amarachi revealed her inner conflict and eventual resolution, Ifeoma's face changed from curiosity to comprehension.

"Have you changed your feelings for him?" Ifeoma's voice was filled with a soft curiosity and a hint of sadness.

Amarachi locked eyes with her friend, her gaze revealing a blend of feelings. *"Well, there's nothing special about his visit, Ifeoma; we just talked, and everyone went his way." I felt it would be rude not to give him an audience since he only came to say hi."*

Ifeoma nodded thoughtfully, receiving Amarachi's words with a composed demeanour. *"Life has a way of surprising us, doesn't it?"* she murmured softly, displaying profound empathy.

Their discussion continued well into noon, with the bond of their friendship helping them navigate through the transition from doubt to understanding. Sharing their thoughts and feelings brought a peaceful connection, strengthening their bond through honesty and trust.

Meanwhile, a week later, Mr Ejiofor and his kinsmen received a visit from Mr Linus' kinsmen in the afternoon. He welcomed them by presenting them with kola nuts. The air was thick with cultural traditions surrounding the presentation of the kola nuts by the hosts.

The kola nuts were broken and eaten at the end of the celebratory speeches and rituals. Then, the oldest man among Mr Linus' kinsmen cleared his throat and said, *"May you see no sudden death!"*

"May you also see no sudden death!" They all chorused and fixed their eyes on the lanky, wiry old man.

"Well," he continued, *"the toad does not run at noon in vain. As a matter of fact, when a child is crying and pointing, look closely; either of the parents is present. We all know that a good commodity market itself."*

"So it is, Nna Anyi." One of his kinsmen provided support.

"It is said that a good road brings about more travel on it. It is our hope that this road we're travelling will induce more travel!" As he sat down, he gestured to Mr Linus to present the keg of palm wine to the host, which he promptly did.

Mr Ejiofor and his kinsmen exchanged glances and then looked back at the visitors.

The old man again cleared his throat and said, *"Our host, this wine belongs to you."* He then sat down quietly, leaning his cheek against his left hand.

"We have received the wine." Mr Ejiofor spoke calmly and sent for tumblers. When the tumblers were brought, Mr Ejiofor asked the youngest among them to pour out the wine, but first to the presenter. The young man poured a glass for Mr Linus, who drank with relish; he then poured for himself, the host, and then for everybody.

When everyone had each taken a glass, Mr Ejiofo cleared his

throat and asked, *"What is this wine meant for?"* His voice was dignified.

They expressed Mr Linus' desire to marry Amarachi!

"We have heard what you said. However, our only response at this point is that you will leave now and go into the house of thinking while we, too, go into the house of consultation."

"Well said," The lanky, wiry old man said they exchanged pleasantries once again and departed.

Later that evening, Mr. Ejiofor made his way to his mother's house and discovered his two brothers already assembled there, anticipating his arrival. Meanwhile, in her room, Amarachi became aware of her father's presence through the sound of his voice. She contemplated stepping out to welcome him but hesitated upon hearing additional voices in the parlour. Intrigued, her curiosity piqued, she remained in her room and involuntarily listened in. What she overheard left her completely incredulous.

Tension filled the air as Mr Ejiofor confronted his brothers, their faces displaying unwavering determination.

"You must grasp the significance of this union," one of the brothers declared, his voice heavy with anticipation. *"Mr Linus hails from a distinguished lineage, and this union would surely elevate our family's reputation."*

Mr Ejiofor stood tall, his gaze steady. *"Regardless of our family background, my daughter's happiness is my top priority. We will not compel her to enter a marriage against her will. Someone suddenly appears from somewhere and declares, "I want to marry your daughter, and this is your position."*

Speaking more forcefully, the second brother interrupted, *"But* it's tradition, Ejiofor." Amarachi's marriage is not entirely up to her; the family decides and approves who she marries.

Mr Ejiofor's jaw clenched, his determination unwavering. "I'm glad you said it, but it's not entirely hers, which means her consent is extremely important." Furthermore, when did this tradition, which I don't know about, begin? Traditions no longer constrain women to choose their own paths, except for the one you imported today. I refuse to pressure my daughter into a marriage she does not desire." "I'm only here to find out whether she had any prior knowledge of this visit today."

Their mother did not utter a word but calmly listened to the arguments and counterarguments. The debate continued, with each party unwavering in their convictions, the conflict between tradition and personal freedom resounding through their mother's residence.

Amarachi stormed out of her room, furious at not being part of the crucial decision-making process.

When Amarachi's father delivered the news, her reaction was not at all what he had anticipated. An intense argument broke out as Amarachi confronted her father for neglecting her and her sister before suddenly arranging her marriage at a young age.

"Father, this is unjust! Amarachi protested, her voice brimming with emotion. *"You can't simply decide on my future without asking me; I must pursue further education. I am not prepared for marriage!"* Amarachi's voice reverberated through the compound, filled with frustration and indignation.

Her father let out a heavy sigh, his tired eyes clearly showing the burden of the situation. *"Amarachi, what have you been filling your head with that you've lost your manners to the point of talking to me this way?"* He confronted her with his eyes, demanding an apology.

"Has it been your decision to send yourself to school and pay the bills all these years?" The decision to pursue further education is yours now, right? So, on whose shoulders does the responsibility rest?"

Amarachi's uncles intervened with firm voices, their faces reflecting a mix of tradition and expectation.

"*Amarachi, you have a responsibility to maintain our family's reputation and values. Marriage is inevitable for women, and you will embrace it regardless of your feelings,*" Alozie, the second uncle, said, his words echoing centuries of customs.

Amarachi's frustration reached its peak as she shook her head in disbelief. *"But what about my dreams? What lies ahead for me?"* She argued, her voice brimming with urgency.

As her father looked at her, he saw nothing but the face of his late wife. A touch of pain appeared in his eyes, softening his expression. *"Amarachi, listen to me. We always have your best interests at heart, which is why we're all here to learn about your position in this whole thing. As you claim, we have not made any decisions without your input. Now I want to ask you: do you know this man? And who is he to you? I don't know him, but your uncles appear to have some information about him."*

"But, father, there's over twenty years' age gap between me and Mr Linus!" "I can't marry someone almost as old as you!" Amarachi's frustration spilt into the conversation as she narrated all she knew about Mr Linus.

"There are times when we need to make tough decisions for the greater good," he whispered, his voice filled with acceptance. *"When a woman reaches a certain age, people often label her as "father will marry her," a fate I wouldn't wish upon you, my*

daughter." Mr Ejiofor, torn between tradition and his daughter's aspirations, tried to reason with her. *"Amarachi, Mr Linus is a good man by the look of things." "He respects our family and can provide for you." Always remember that the respect you have as a woman is your husband."*

Alozie fixed Amarachi with a steady gaze that left her confused before speaking up, *"Amarachi, whatever position we have taken in this matter is purely based on your prompting."* He darted his protuberant eyes from her to the rest of the people, then back at her again.

"How do you mean, Uncle?" She stuttered.

"The movement of legs with ankle bells is watched by eyes with goggle lenses." He nodded to Iwundu, the first uncle to talk.

"You said you're not yet ready to marry, right? Then, why were you wiggling your waist and stomach on the mound by the Achi tree the other day?"

Amarachi's mind went blank. *"I was only carried away by the performance of my friends!"* she cried in exasperation.

"Do you know how many eyes saw you?" He continued, *"For the past six years, we have stood firmly behind you and warded off all approaches for two basic reasons: first, you were too young for marriage, and second, your stand was very clear to us all. Now that you have openly declared your readiness, how do you blame us?"*

"Amarachi, I want to ask you one question," Alozie spoke up again. *"Can you honestly, from the bottom of your heart, tell us that you have not taken a liking to this Linus?" If not, how do you explain the hilarious atmosphere around the primary school a week ago? In effect, all we're saying is: Give us a stand to take when these people*

come knocking again. You see, a child scrubs only the belly when asked to bathe. We're only trying to guide you, right? Nobody here hates you. It's all for your best interest."

The pressure to marry and uphold the family lineage weighed heavily on Amarachi's shoulders, a burden compounded by the whispers of the kinsmen and the weight of tradition. Their voices echoed in the corridors of her mind, their expectations casting a shadow over her hopes and dreams.

Amarachi felt a wave of despair wash over her as she came to terms with her situation. Struggling to balance tradition with her personal dreams, she understood that the road ahead would be difficult and demanding. However, a spark of defiance flickered deep within her, reminding her of the strength and resilience in her heart.

Grandma, who had been silently observing, intervened at this point. *"Amarachi, times are changing. Mr. Linus is willing to support your education. Marriage doesn't mean the end of your dreams; it can be the beginning of a new chapter. There are several women today who reached the peak of their educational career just because they got married to the man who supported them."* Amarachi came under the scrutiny of her eyes as she spoke. *"I have looked at your hips, and I can confidently tell you that you won't have any problems with childbearing. You grew up here under my watch, and I also know you're mentally sound. You have nothing to worry about."*

The conversation continued, with emotions swirling like a turbulent river. Amarachi, torn between tradition and her aspirations, faced a decision that would shape the course of her future. The air was thick with tension, cultural expectations, and the clash of generations. As the sun dipped below the horizon, the outcome of this familial battle remained uncertain, hanging in the balance of tradition, dreams, and the enduring ties that bound them together.

Upon the second visit of Mr. Linus and his kinsmen, Amarachi gave her consent by accepting Mr. Linus' proposal gift in the presence of the two parties. After this, Mr Linus and his kinsmen pleaded that the other steps should be merged together so that he could finish quickly and return to his base.

Mr. Ejiofor's compound and Grandma's house became a beehive of activities for Amarachi's *gbankwùnwanyi* (traditional wedding). Towards evening, the compound overflowed with people as Mr Linus' kinsmen gathered to fulfil the ancient customs stated in the list before Amarachi could be his wife. The air was thick with a mixture of tradition, excitement, and the ceremonial gestures that bound the community together.

Chief Okorie, representing Mr Ejiofor's family, stood proudly in the middle of the gathering as he welcomed the kinsmen. The negotiation, laden with symbolism, began with the elders engaging in spirited discussions over the appropriate amount of palm wine and other things the age-long tradition demanded.

Once all was deemed satisfactory, the formal ceremony commenced. Amarachi, adorned in traditional attire, was escorted by Ifeoma, who was also elegantly dressed, along with Ngozi and other maidens, to welcome the guests. As she caught sight of Mr Linus, their exchanged glances spoke volumes, his eyes reflecting a blend of pride and gratitude for the unity being celebrated.

As the negotiations reached a harmonious conclusion, Amarachi was called out again and given a cup filled with wine.

"Are you asking us to drink this wine?" her kinsmen asked. She nodded with a smile and everywhere erupted in cheers.

"In that case, take a sip and go and give it to the one you know is your husband."

Amarachi took a sip and stepped forward in obedience, but not without the novelty of first walking around as if searching for Mr Linus. When she finally got to where he was, she kneeled and offered him the wine. Everybody cheered again and applauded.

Mr Linus, on his own part, received the cup of wine, took a sip, and passed it over to the eldest man among his kinsmen. When everyone had had a sip, signifying unity of purpose, the cup finally returned to Mr Linus, who gladly gulped down the rest.

Chief Okorie, together with her kinsmen, prayed and blessed Amarachi, saying, *"You are now part of Linus' family. "May your union with him be fruitful, and may you find joy and fulfilment in your new home."*

This marked the climax of the ceremony. As the symbolic calabash, signifying fertility and prosperity, was presented to her, symbolizing her transition into a new life with Mr Linus and her elevated status, tears streamed down her cheeks uncontrollably despite her efforts to restrain them. Ngozi, her sister, stood by her side, joined by Ifeoma and several others, offering their support during this emotional moment.

Eventually, it was time to go, and Ifeoma smiled laconically and watched longingly as her friend was taken away by Mr Linus. There was no denying that she played a role in this union and whatever outcome it might hold in the future.

Chapter Three:
Amarachi in a New World

Days later, as they made arrangements for their departure, Amarachi experienced a whirlwind of mixed emotions. Her conversations with her grandmother were imbued with wisdom and blessings. "Amarachi, you bear the aspirations of our family to this foreign land. May you bring honour to us, my dear child."

The journey from the village to Lagos was a testament to the interconnectedness of tradition and modernity. That was the very first time Amarachi would travel to Lagos. The twelve-hour drive was indeed tiring for the new couple. The driver drove them straight to the Sheraton Hotel in Ikeja, Lagos so that they could navigate to the airport the following day.

On the plane, as they soared above the clouds, Mr Linus sought to ease Amarachi's nerves with conversations. *"Amarachi, this is the beginning of our shared adventure. London awaits us with new opportunities and experiences."*

Amarachi, gazing out of the window, replied, *"I am ready for this new chapter, Dede. It's a bit overwhelming, but I trust that we'll navigate it together."*

Upon landing at Heathrow Airport, Mr Linus' friend, Obi, came to pick them up. Amarachi, feeling a blend of excitement and apprehension, engaged in a conversation with him about what to expect. *"London is different from our village, but you'll adapt. Mr Linus has told me so much about you, Amarachi."* He stated.

During the car journey from Heathrow Terminal 5 to southeast London, Mr Linus enthusiastically pointed out various landmarks and attractions, demonstrating his extensive local knowledge.

"Look, that's Buckingham Palace," Mr. Linus exclaimed eagerly, gesturing towards the magnificent building as they drove by. *"It's where Queen Elizabeth resided before her passing. Quite a spectacle, wouldn't you agree?"*

Amarachi nodded, her eyes widening in awe at the majestic structure. *"This is absolutely amazing,"* she whispered, her voice tinged with awe.

With every new discovery, Amarachi was filled with wonder, yet a lingering sense of unease lurked beneath her enthusiasm.

London seemed to be a completely different world from anything she had experienced before; despite its beauty and grandeur, she felt the weight of the unfamiliar surroundings, which dimmed the thrill of discovery.

Mr Linus observed her discomfort and gave her a comforting smile. *"London may seem a bit daunting at first, but you'll get the hang of it soon. There is an abundance of sights and activities to explore, ensuring you will never experience a dull moment,"* he comforted, with a reassuring and inviting tone.

Amarachi nodded appreciatively in response to his encouraging words. As the car journeyed ahead, she felt a blend of anticipation and nervousness stirring inside her—a feeling of exploration coloured by the unpredictability of what lay ahead. This feeling continued as the car stopped on Castello Street, off Old Kent Road in Peckham.

Arriving at Mr Linus' rented two-bedroom flat in southeast

London, Amarachi observed the humble exterior of the council house. It was a high-rise council block of flats that was built in the Victorian era. The aged red brick façade and flaking paint indicated years of neglect. The cracked, weathered, deep blue communal entrance door sagged loosely on its hinges, its previous majesty gone. The little front yard was now unenclosed by the corroded and twisted railings. The walkway was obstructed by overgrown weeds and messy hedges, and the area was further degraded by pieces of rubbish.

The contrast between the village and the urban landscape was evident and became immediately apparent upon Amarachi alighting from Mr Obi's Toyota Prius car. She couldn't help but experience a twinge of disappointment; during their conversations in the village, Mr Linus had painted such a rosy picture of his city life. She had anticipated a more refined atmosphere, one that reflected the dignified demeanour that Mr Linus exhibited in the village. However, while they awaited the lift to the fourth floor of the building, she was unable to mask the foul odour emanating from the corridor. Mr Linus guided Amarachi through the narrow hallway, his voice filled with pride as he gave her a tour of the humble apartment.

Upon entering the two-bedroom flat, the pleasant and comfortable atmosphere of the apartment encircled Amarachi like a cosy blanket. In the living room, the aged armchair near the fireplace beckoned for a moment of rest, its fabric worn smooth from years of usage. A faded rug with elaborate designs served as an anchor for the sitting area, while an antique coffee table was tucked away among a scatter of mismatched couches. There were pictures of Mr Linus and some paintings on the walls.

Stepping into the cosy kitchen, Mr Linus showed Amarachi how to operate the cooking gas and assisted her in arranging all the ingredients and foodstuffs they brought from Nigeria.

"I need to go back to work," Mr Obi stated after ensuring there was nothing more he could help the new couples with. *"I will check on you people tomorrow,"* he concluded as he headed off to his car to continue his taxi business.

Mr Linus guided Amarachi into the bedrooms—one containing only a single bed and a small desk—where Obi, who brought them from the airport, lived before moving out two weeks ago when he realised Linus would be coming back with his new wife. The master bedroom was furnished with a delightful assortment of historical furniture and treasured souvenirs, each of which had a unique tale to tell.

Amarachi nodded in understanding, feeling a sense of warmth from the belongings that filled the humble abode. Although not flawless, she saw the flat as symbolising the potential for fresh starts—a space where aspirations could grow and relationships could thrive amid urban activity.

As she embraced her new environment, Amarachi felt grateful for the opportunity to begin a new chapter in her life as she unloaded her personal belongings in the master bedroom.

Mr Linus called Amarachi's father, and when the line connected, he exchanged a few pleasantries with him and handed the phone over to Amarachi.

"Good evening, papa," she began. *"How is everybody? Ngozi nwanne m kwanù?, na Nnenkukwu? Please help me tell her that I'm fine, that I'll try to call whenever I can, and that you are around to tell her about my affairs. Extend my greetings to Ifeoma."* The conversation was brief and dwelt more on her trip to London and other trifles.

Over time, as Amarachi settled into her role as a full-time housewife, Mr Linus continued to support and guide her through the nuances of London life. Their conversations evolved from the challenges of adaptation to the dreams and aspirations they held for their future.

Cultural differences became a bridge, not a barrier, as they navigated the intricacies of a new world. In her own way, Amarachi became a bridge between the traditions she brought from the village and the endless opportunities London offered.

The following weekend, Mr Linus took Amarachi sightseeing through central London.

"Look at this picture, Mr Linus, "*Amarachi said, handing him her phone and a snapshot of Covent Garden.* "Isn't it incredible?"

Mr Linus laughed quietly. *"Please, Amarachi, don't address me as 'Mr Linus'. "You can just call me Linus."*

Amarachi paused, a small flush spreading over her cheeks. "*I... I know, it's just... the age gap, you know?"*

Linus smiled fondly and reached for her hand. *"Darling, age is only a number. What is important is the bond we share as husband and wife.".*

Amarachi grinned back, softly grasping his hand. *"I know you're correct, L...L. Linus. "It just takes some time to get used to it."*

Mr Linus looked at the photograph, a smile spreading across his face... *"Absolutely gorgeous, Amarachi. Covent Garden is usually bustling with life."*

"And wait until you see these flower stall pictures," she said

eagerly. *"They're like something out of a fairy tale."*

"I'm glad you're having fun," Mr Linus replied cheerfully. *"It's a pleasure to show you around the city."*

As they reached London Bridge, Amarachi looked at Mr Linus, her eyes filled with admiration. *"I can't believe we're really here, Mr Linus. "It feels surreal."*

Mr Linus nodded, his eyes soaking in the magnificent sight of the bridge. *"It's a symbol of resilience and history, standing strong through the ages."*

Amarachi smiled in gratitude for the experience. *"Thanks for bringing me here, Mr Linus." It means a lot to me".*

"It's my pleasure, Amarachi," he said, his tone warm. *"I'm glad I could share this moment with you."* He concluded as they made their way to the London Bridge train station to catch a train back home.

Ngozi and Ifeoma were so glad when Amarachi forwarded some of the pictures to them. They were so particular about the ones she took near the London Bridge and asked her if the *"London Bridge is falling down"* song was true!

As the days turned into weeks, their shared journey unfolded, marked by conversations that weaved together their union. The challenges of adaptation became shared triumphs, and through it all, Amarachi and Mr Linus discovered that their love and understanding could bridge any gap, making their journey more profound and meaningful than they could have imagined.

The evenings in Mr. Linus' modest home were filled with the echoes of their dreams, aspirations, and the occasional clash of perspectives. One such evening, as the golden hues of the setting sun painted their surroundings, Mr. Linus was off work, and Amarachi broached a subject that had been weighing on her heart.

"Dede," Amarachi called her husband. *I've been thinking about my education. I want to further my studies before we start having our children. I am sure you know quite well that I was waiting for my WAEC to be released before my kinsmen gave me to you in marriage."*

Mr Linus responded with a smile that held both warmth and hesitation. *"Amarachi, I've asked you to stop referring to me as Dede. I am your husband, not your uncle or elder brother,"* he retorted, a hint of frustration edging into his tone.

"But you are old enough to be my father," Amarachi countered gently. *"You are well aware of our tradition; it's expected that I address someone who is old enough to be my father with respect. You know, Dede, there is a significant age gap of twenty years between us."*

Mr Linus nodded in understanding, his attention now fully on her inquiry. *"I appreciate your aspirations and your eagerness to learn,"* he began, his tone gentle yet resolute. *"However, I believe our priority at the moment should be building our family. Education can certainly be pursued at a later time, my dear."*

The air seemed to be still as Amarachi's hopeful eyes met Mr Linus' resolute gaze. It was a moment pregnant with unspoken desires and conflicting visions of the future. Amarachi, though understanding, felt a tinge of disappointment as the pursuit of her educational dreams seemed to slip further away.

Weeks turned into months, and the undercurrents of their differing priorities remained, subtly shaping the contours of their daily lives. Amarachi could not understand why a man who had been in the UK for years could not see any other work to do than to secure a supermarket!

Unknown to her, Mr Linus was a chameleon who never honoured his commitments; every agreement he made was driven by selfish motives. With limited formal education, he had navigated a path shaped by the exigencies of his ambition. His life took a dramatic turn when his master sent him to the UK on a business errand, an opportunity that altered his destiny. Opting not to return, he found himself undertaking various menial jobs, a journey characterised by resilience but fraught with the challenges of surviving in a world vastly different from the comforts of his village.

In addition to his struggles, Chief Chukwudi, his master, demanded that he return the funds intended for purchasing motor spare parts, which he had diverted for personal use. They managed to resolve the issue amicably, with Mr. Linus agreeing to return a portion of the misused funds to Chief Chukwudi. This resolution helped to ease the conflict between them. To stabilize his residency in the UK, Mr. Linus entered into an arranged marriage with an Eastern European woman who was eighteen years older than him—a hellish five-year union that felt like an eternity. It was only after he became a British citizen that he filed for divorce, which now freed him to travel to Nigeria to marry Amarachi.

"Why then did he brag about coming from London at the venue of the Nkaonu festival when he is a mere security officer?" She pondered. She saw clearly from Mr. Linus' eyes that he was not ready to see her go to school, and she, on her part, was not ready to get pregnant. In her naivety, she started coming up with one illness or another whenever Mr. Linus came near her, but she knew deep down that it would only be a temporary measure.

Amarachi woke up one morning with an uncomfortable sensation in her tummy as the sun coloured the sky pink and gold. The soft sunshine coming through the curtains provided little comfort as she was overwhelmed with a strong feeling of illness. When she tried to get out of bed, she had a sudden round of morning sickness, causing her to feel anxious and shaky.

The persistent nausea was a constant reminder of the internal turmoil she was experiencing, intensifying her feeling of unease. Amarachi was alone in the morning, dealing with the heaviness of doubt, her pulse resounding in the silence.

Amarachi's head was filled with swirling questions, each one filled with worry and mistrust. *"Is it possible? Did the symptoms she had suggest pregnancy?"* The idea caused her to feel a strong sense of fear, emphasising the seriousness of the issue.

For the first time, Amarachi faced a new vulnerability as the world outside began to awaken. Initially a distant idea, the possibility of becoming a mother suddenly appeared prominently in her future, causing uncertainty about her well-thought-out plans.

Amarachi took a pregnancy test at the General Practice the day after Mr Linus suggested it. The surprise came with the test result: positive! Amarachi had a mix of astonishment, delight, and mild worry as she held the test in her hands.

Mr Linus beamed with joy. *"Amarachi, we're going to be parents! This is wonderful news, my love."*

Amarachi's intentions of advancing her studies and achieving her objectives were overshadowed by the enormous anxiety of parenting, despite Mr Linus' promises and their deep relationship. She struggled with conflicting feelings in her peaceful thoughts, torn between the prospect of a fresh life and the intimidating uncertainty that awaited her.

On their way home in Mr Linus' black Toyota Corolla car, Amarachi couldn't suppress the nagging thought of the dreams that seemed to drift further away. In the quiet moments that followed, their conversation wove through the complexities of their intertwined destinies.

"Amarachi, I noticed your expression changed when the nurse mentioned you are pregnant. Aren't you happy that we're going to be parents soon?" he asked as they sat in their living room.

"Dede, I am happy about the baby, but I can't help but think about my dreams. I still want to further my studies, and now it feels like it's slipping away even more," Amarachi confessed, her eyes reflecting a mix of joy and inner turmoil.

Mr Linus, torn between the joy of impending parenthood and the understanding of Amarachi's aspirations, replied, *"Amarachi, I want to give our child the best, and that includes a stable family. Let's focus on building that foundation first, and then we can consider other plans. Education is important, but so is our family."*

Their words hung in the air, a delicate dance of emotions and differing visions for the future. The joy of new life mingled with the unspoken complexities of their journey, a journey where the threads of family, dreams, and compromises were intricately woven into the fabric of their shared destiny.

The nine months of Amarachi's pregnancy became a mixture of emotions, intricately woven with both joy and struggle. Navigating the uncharted waters of motherhood, she grappled with the changes in her body, the nuances of prenatal care, and the sheer newness of the experience.

One evening, Mr Linus sat beside Amarachi, their hands entwined. She turned to him, her eyes reflecting both excitement and apprehension. "Dede, do you think I'll be a good mother? I feel so many things right now."

Mr Linus, with a reassuring smile, replied, "Amarachi, you'll be a wonderful mother. We'll figure this out together, step by step.

Two weeks after their discussion, Amarachi woke up in the morning and started breathing heavily. My Linus was getting ready to go to work when he heard Amarachi's voice from the toilet.

"Dede," she shouted. "*I believe it is time.* "The contractions are becoming stronger and closer together."

"There is no time to waste; I need to tell my employer that I won't be able to come to work today and get you to the hospital." He said it in a worried but calm manner.

"We need to go to Lewisham Hospital right away."

Do you have everything ready in your hospital bag?"

She nodded, wincing with another contraction. "Yes, it is near the entrance door. Let's go quickly."

Linus helped Amarachi get inside the car, guiding her gently. "I'll drive as fast and safely as I can."

Amarachi grimaced despite the discomfort. Thank you, Linus. "I can't believe it's actually happening."

"You're doing well, Amarachi. "We'll be at the hospital soon," he promised her, his voice firm.

Linus raced into Lewisham Hospital and talked hurriedly with the receptionist. "My wife is in labour. Her contractions are around five minutes apart. "This is her first pregnancy."

The receptionist smiled professionally. *"We will bring her to the maternity ward right now. "A nurse will be here to help you."*

A nurse approached with a wheelchair. *Hello, my name is Nurse Margaret. Let's get you to a delivery room. Just take deep breaths and try to stay calm".*

"Thank you, Nurse Margaret," Amarachi said, appreciative of the help.

In the delivery room, Nurse Margaret checked monitors and IVs with efficiency and reassurance. *"Everything looks great, Amarachi. You are making good progress. "I am going to call the doctor right now."*

Moments later, the doctor entered the room. *"Hi, Amarachi. I am Dr. Sonia. "How do you feel?"*

"It hurts, but I'm managing," Amarachi said, fighting through another contraction.

Dr. Sonia offered her a comforting smile. *"You're doing well. Let's see how far along you are."*

Linus clasped Amarachi's hand, his eyes full of awe. *"You're quite powerful, Amarachi. "I am right here with you."*

She clasped his hand to get strength from his presence. *"Thank you".*

"Amarachi, you're fully dilated," Dr. Sonia said. *"It is time to start pushing. Nurse Margaret and I are here to help you."*

Nurse Margaret positioned herself. *"On the next contraction, I want you to take a deep breath and push as hard as you can."*

Amarachi nodded with conviction in her eyes. *"Okay, I can do this."*

Linus leaned forward and spoke encouragingly. *"You can do it, Amarachi. Simply breathe and push."*

As the contraction began, Amarachi pushed with all her effort. "Ahhhh!"

"Great job, Amarachi!" Doctor Sonia exclaimed. *"I see the head." "Just a couple more pushes."*

"You're doing well. "Keep going," Nurse Margaret said.

Amarachi, fatigued but resolute, nodded. *"I can feel it... almost there."*

"One more big push, Amarachi!" Dr. Sonia encouraged.

Amarachi gave it her best in the end. *"Ahhhhh!"*

"Here the baby comes!" Nurse Margaret stated this while holding the newborn baby.

"Congratulations, Amarachi and Linus," Dr. Sonia replied, smiling broadly. *"You have a beautiful baby boy."*

Amarachi's eyes welled with tears of delight. *"I can't believe it. He's finally here."*

Linus kissed her forehead, his eyes full of pride. *"You did it, Amarachi." He's gorgeous, exactly like you.*

After cleaning the baby, Nurse Margaret put the baby in Amarachi's chest. *"Here you go, mom." Meet your son."*

Amarachi embraced the baby carefully, her heart full of love.

Hello, tiny one. *"Welcome to the world."*

Linus grinned, his heart filled. *"Welcome, truly."* Our family is complete."

"Congratulations again," Nurse Margaret remarked quietly. *"We will allow you some time to connect with your baby. If you need anything, please let us know."*

"Well done, Amarachi. You performed an outstanding job. Enjoy this amazing time." Dr. Sonia said as she walked out of the delivery room.

Amarachi glanced up at Linus, her eyes full of appreciation. *"Thank you for everything, Dede."*

Linus' voice was sweet as he said, *"No, thank you, Amarachi. You have given us the greatest gift of all, a baby boy!"*

Amarachi was discharged the following day, and they all went back home.

The village of Amufigbo resounded with jubilation upon hearing that Amarachi had given birth to a baby boy. Mr. Ejiofor, Amarachi's father, was particularly elated, knowing his daughter wouldn't endure the pressures her mother faced from her in-laws. Mr. Linus was filled with joy at the arrival of his child, cherishing the new life he had brought into the world. As Amarachi cradled her new born, the weight of tradition intertwined with the bliss of motherhood within her. In moments of quiet reflection, she couldn't help but trace her aspirations with delicate fingers, pondering when the pursuit of her education would find its place in her life.

Days turned into months, and the struggles of early motherhood unfolded. Late at night, as Mr Linus rocked their son to sleep, Amarachi would gaze into the darkness, contemplating her dreams and aspirations.

One day, she mustered the courage to voice her desires: *"Dede, I've been thinking about my education. I want to further my studies; I never thought of becoming a mother before getting my degree, and that was why I stayed away from men in the village"*.

Mr Linus, with a smile laced with both warmth and hesitation, replied, *"Amarachi, I understand your aspirations, and I appreciate your eagerness to learn. But right now, I think our focus should be on taking care of our little boy. Education can come later, my dear."*

The air seemed to be still as their eyes locked, each silently wrestling with their own expectations and visions for the future. The clash of perspectives hung in the room, an unspoken tension beneath the surface.

Amarachi's head was filled with ideas for her studies, her ambitions fluttering like illusive butterflies in the garden of her dreams.

Barely six months after the arrival of their son, Amarachi was disheartened to learn that she was expecting another child. The news overwhelmed her like a powerful tidal wave, erasing the joy of being a new mother and replacing it with a profound feeling of fear and anxiety. She sat on the side of their bed, holding the positive pregnancy test, her hands quivering, tears brimming in her eyes.

"Dede," she said, her voice faltering, *"I... I am pregnant again."*

Linus, who was adjusting their son's cot, turned around slowly; his eyes sparkled with delight as a grin stretched across his face. *"Amarachi, that's fantastic news!"* he exclaimed enthusiastically.

"Another child, another blessing to our family."

Amarachi's thoughts drifted towards her aspirations of starting her education as he held her. With the impending arrival of another child, such aspirations seemed to be further out of reach.

Unknown to her, Linus had planned to get her pregnant again, hoping to shatter her ambitions and keep her bound as a full housewife.

Amarachi couldn't suppress a hint of a let down at Mr Linus' eager response.

As those words re-echoed in her mind, Amarachi's heart sank under the burden of missed opportunities and shattered dreams. She was determined to continue her education, but Mr Linus appeared to have different priorities. It never occurred to her that he was an opportunist who had no interest in her pursuit of education; rather, his intentions were grounded in his longing for companionship with a young woman with whom he could establish a family.

As she grappled with her thoughts, the concept of abortion danced in her mind like a flickering flame in the distance. However, her cultural beliefs and upbringing as a Catholic restrained her, keeping her on a path she was uncertain about.

Chapter Four:
Beyond The Veil

Amarachi could hear the ôjaas, a distant sound that grew louder and louder. *"There's a way around every difficulty,"* the ôja said. She sighed heavily, and her eyes lit up.

"That ogre felt it had the upper hand, relying on his formidable strength and influence, but... he was defeated by a little girl. How? Fight till your last breath; never give up. Defeat and death only occur when you surrender."

Those were the ôja's motivational words to her and her teammates, which moved them into a frenzy in a dancing competition the moment they were getting tired. And they had the last laugh at the end of the day.

Amarachi's mind became very clear about the situation. She felt as though a veil had lifted from her mind. Mr. Linus' excitement was simply an expression of victory. His strategy was to frustrate her aspirations by getting her pregnant. She became more resolute than ever, determined to take advantage of the situation to the best of her ability.

She immersed herself in online research, exploring various colleges in her vicinity. Despite being academically qualified to enter the university directly based on her WAEC results, Amarachi believed that enrolling in Access to Social Work would provide a deeper understanding of the UK educational system.

Remarkably, just two months into her second pregnancy,

Amarachi secured admission to study Access to Social Work at the London South East College. She was determined to complete the six-month course before giving birth to her second child.

On the evening of the day she received the admission news, Amarachi gathered her courage, preparing herself to face Mr. Linus' reaction as she disclosed her plans. She began, *"Dede, I have some important news to share with you. I've been granted admission to study in the Access to Social Work programme at the London South East College."*

Mr Linus' brows furrowed in astonishment, with disappointment written all over his face. *"Amarachi,"* he said with a hint of exasperation, *"haven't we already talked about this?" We had previously discussed the importance of prioritising our growing family at this time."*

Amarachi locked eyes with him, her determination unwavering. *"I get your worries, Dede,"* she responded calmly, *"but continuing my education is crucial to me. "I am confident that I can balance my studies with my duties as a wife and mother."*

Mr Linus let out a heavy sigh, clearly showing his disappointment. *"You're quite stubborn, Amarachi,"* he said, shaking his head. *"If that's really what you want, I'll be there for you, even if I have a different perspective."*

That was how Linus reluctantly agreed to allow Amarachi to pursue her dreams. Amarachi experienced a wave of relief and determination. She was prepared to begin this new phase of her life, determined to follow her dreams despite the obstacles that lay ahead. Amarachi, juggling between motherhood and academia, threw herself into her coursework with a fervour that mirrored her internal resolve. She was lucky to find a woman to babysit her son. Mrs Afolabi, who lived in the same council flats, had come from Nigeria to spend a few months with her son, and she decided to use that opportunity to get extra cash. It was a huge relief to Amarachi.

With the birth of her second child, a son, Amarachi's life became even more complex. Managing her expanding family while also pursuing her academic goals became increasingly difficult. Despite the increased duties, Amarachi stayed resolute. Thriving in her Access to Social Work programme, she gained acceptance to the University of East London to study Social Work. Nevertheless, she decided to postpone her enrolment for a year, understanding the importance of focusing on her family responsibilities before continuing her education.

Amarachi found juggling parenting and studying difficult, but it paid off. Learning remotely from home as a result of the COVID lockdown allowed her to dedicate more time to looking after her sons. This not only reduced the responsibility of childcare costs but also gave her the valuable opportunity to be with her children at home. The flexibility allowed her to manage her responsibilities as a mother while pursuing her studies, which she enjoyed throughout her three-year course.

With a degree in social work, she embraced her role, orchestrating the delicate dance of family and career in their southeast London flat. Amarachi's increasing success in her career brought financial prosperity, but it also stirred unanticipated feelings in her husband.

During this period, she maintained regular communication with Grandma and Ngozi, occasionally sending them tokens from the maintenance fund she had received as a student. She also re-established regular and long telephone conversations with Ifeoma, who by this time was the mistress of her own hairdressing salon.

The family was relatively stable until the end of the COVID-19 pandemic. However, an undercurrent of trouble had been brewing and was about to erupt with every passing moment. Mr Linus' inadequacies were coming to light with Amarachi's maturation; her much more advanced education and larger income kept him on edge and made him feel like a toothless bulldog.

One evening, a silent tension pervaded the living room. Mr. Linus paused before articulating his thoughts: "Amarachi, I've been pondering. If I had furthered my studies, perhaps my circumstances would have been different today.

Amarachi, placing her bag on the table, met his gaze with understanding. *"Dede, you gave me the chance to study, and now we're both contributing to our family. We're a team, and your role is just as vital. Besides, it's not too late to do that; at least that will relieve you of the security job you have been doing for years"*

Linus hesitated for a moment and said, *"Where would I start at this age?"*

As days stretched into weeks, Mr. Linus' unease deepened. The awareness that Amarachi's monthly earnings surpassed his own began to gnaw at him, prompting introspection. Caught between admiration for his wife's accomplishments and a lingering feeling of inadequacy, he stood at a crossroads. With each passing moment, a new narrative unfolded, bringing forth an unforeseen turn of events. Formerly the primary breadwinner, Mr. Linus now wrestled with a disquiet he struggled to put into words. Yet, beneath her words, a subtle shift occurred. Mr Linus, once the mentor, grappled with a sense of inadequacy, questioning his choices and pondering alternate paths.

Amarachi had barely settled into her work as a social worker with the Westminster City Council when the government relaxed COVID-related restrictions. This made her work in the office

Monday through Friday. Amarachi had just gone to pick up the children from the childminder and was surprised to meet Mr Linus at home.

Mr Linus felt a heavy burden of impending news as he entered his house. The sound of each step resonated with the significance of the occasion; the well-known crack of the floorboards broke the heavy silence in the room. The walls appeared to be closing in on him, intensifying the tightness building up in his chest. As he walked, the burden of doubt weighed heavily on him, creating strange shadows that moved menacingly on the walls. He felt a strong sensation of fear as he neared the centre of his house, where his family was sitting. His heart was beating rapidly against his ribs. He prepared himself for the challenging discussion ahead, certain that the words he was about to speak would have a lasting impact on their lives.

Mr Linus continued solemnly, "Amarachi, we had a meeting today." His words lingered in the air, charging the atmosphere with expectation. *"The pandemic is causing the company to reduce its workforce, and unfortunately, my job is among those affected."*

Standing beside the kitchen counter, Amarachi felt a surge of anxiety. The news about job uncertainty disturbed their previously solid routine. She said with a worried expression, *"Oh, Dede, I'm deeply sorry to hear that." Do they offer any compensation or support?*

Mr Linus sighed. *"Yes, they're giving a redundancy package, but it's not the same as having a regular income, you know."*

Amarachi stepped closer, extending a reassuring hand. *"We'll navigate this together,"* she assured him, her touch a gesture of solidarity.

"Any idea on the amount?" she inquired casually, her tone masking the underlying concern.

Amarachi was unaware that Mr Linus had a different plan for the redundancy pay. He accepted her reassurance with a grateful smile, concealing the seed of intention growing within him.

Understanding the pandemic's upheaval, the company offered Mr Linus a generous severance package of twenty-five thousand pounds the following day as a lifeline for his redundancy pay and his fourteen years of service to the organisation as a security officer. He was elated despite not knowing what the future had in store for him.

When he got home, he told his wife about the pay-out, and Amarachi remarked, *"We've got some savings, and between my job and what you received, don't you think this is an opportunity for us to make strides in our homeownership journey with this pay-out?"*

Little did she know, Mr Linus' mind was already weaving dreams of a different nature. His intentions went far beyond the family's immediate financial stability.

Weeks drifted by, and the family settled into a fresh routine, adjusting to Amarachi assuming the role of primary breadwinner. Mr. Linus, appearing content with the change, maintained a facade of gratitude for the financial cushion provided by his redundancy package.

Focused on upholding stability, Amarachi remained oblivious to the subtle undercurrents of transformation brewing beneath the surface. As they navigated the ongoing challenges of the pandemic, they remained unaware that a pivotal chapter was unfolding—one destined to reshape the fabric of their lives and introduce unforeseen complexities.

Exactly two months after Mr. Linus received his redundancy payout, within the quiet confines of their bedroom, he broached a subject that would disrupt the tranquillity they had painstakingly nurtured. Beside Amarachi, a palpable hesitancy lingered in the air before he spoke.

"Amarachi, there's something I need to tell you," he began, his voice threading through the silence.

She turned towards him, curious yet unsuspecting. *"What is it, Dede?"*

"I've decided to take a trip to Nigeria," he declared, his words hanging in the air.

Amarachi was caught off guard and sat up, a furrow forming on her brow. *"Nigeria? When? Why?"*

"I've been thinking about it for a while. There are some matters I need to attend to back home," he explained.

"But why now?" We're facing uncertainties here, and this seems sudden," she responded, a tinge of concern in her voice.

Mr Linus, resolute, stated, *"I've made up my mind, Amarachi. There are things I need to handle back home, and now is the right time."*

Perplexed, Amarachi sought to understand. *"But we should have discussed this. "Why didn't you tell me earlier?"*

He nodded decisively, affirming his resolve. *"I understand this comes as a surprise, but it's necessary. I won't be away for long, and I'll return sooner than you think."*

Amarachi, grappling with the unexpected revelation, felt a palpable unease settle in the room. The conversation lingered, with Mr Linus' choice casting a shadow over the stability they had worked hard to maintain amidst challenges.

The next evening, Mr Linus boarded a British Airways flight from Heathrow Terminal 5 to Lagos, Nigeria, leaving Amarachi and the two young boys behind in their South East London flat. It was then that Amarachi realised yet again that they both held differing perceptions about life.

The living room was heavy with unspoken tension as Amarachi and Mr Linus grappled with the unexpected turns of their lives during his return from Nigeria.

Amarachi, furrowing her brow, finally broke the silence. *"Dede, I don't understand. Why did you travel to Nigeria with the redundancy payment? We could have used that money to make a mortgage deposit here in London."*

Mr Linus, seated on the worn-out sofa, sighed heavily before responding, *"Amarachi, it's not that simple. There were expectations and cultural obligations. Building a mansion in the village is something I needed to do, and I know you know how important it is."*

Amarachi's frustration simmered beneath the surface as she retorted, *"But what about our family here? The rented apartment, our bills, and the children's needs loomed large. We needed that money for our lives in London."*

Mr Linus, struggling to explain, tried to convey the weight of tradition: *"You know how it is, Amarachi. It's about respect and fulfilling the expectations of our people. This is something I had to do."* *"I would rather be a tenant in the UK for my lifetime than not have a befitting house in the village."* He stressed.

The echoes of cultural influence reverberated through their conversation, introducing a layer of complexity to their familial dynamics.

"But how come you do not find it worthwhile to discuss all of these with me before you travel home?" So how much is left of the money?" Amarachi pressed, her voice edged with frustration.

Mr Linus, torn between cultural expectations and the reality of their lives in London, responded, *"I understand, Amarachi. I do. But we can navigate this. Our family will be fine. This is an investment in our future."*

The rented apartment, once a symbol of stability, now bears witness to the challenges introduced by Mr Linus' unexpected move. The conversation, a reflection of the shifting dynamics, highlighted the clash between tradition and the pragmatic realities of their lives in London. The very fabric of their story underwent further transformation, woven with the threads of tradition, expectations, and the evolving dynamics of a family caught between two worlds. This left Amarachi and the family in a rented apartment in southeast London, and the echoes of cultural influence reverberated through their lives, introducing new challenges and reshaping the dynamics of their family story.

Amarachi, exhausted by her husband's extended period of inactivity in job hunting, could no longer hide her worries. One evening, while seated in their living room, she brought up the topic with a combination of exasperation and a need for reassurance.

"Dede, are you not bothered by the fact that you have not secured a job yet?" She expressed her pent-up ideas after more than two years.

Mr Linus, reclining on the couch, nonchalantly shrugged. *"I will* surely get a job when the appropriate opportunity presents itself." There is no rush required.

Amarachi persisted, expressing her frustration: "*My dear, we cannot continue to wait.*" *We have obligations, and I cannot sustain being the only provider forever.*

Mr Linus, seeming unperturbed, said, *"Why worry? You are doing an excellent job, and we have everything we need."*.

At that point, Amarachi felt a growing irritation. *"It's not solely about money, Dede. We are creating a life together. Collective responsibilities and aspirations. As the patriarch, the cultural values that led you to build a mansion in Nigeria, a place we may never reside in, also entail being the primary provider for our family. "Dede, demonstrate the qualities of a man that society expects you to possess,"* she sobbed.

His response was a casual assurance that bothered indifference. *"We'll get there, Amarachi. Let's not make a big deal out of it. After all, people in the village are still commending me to date for building such a lovely house within a short time."*

Weeks passed, and the strain on Amarachi's shoulders intensified. In another attempt to convey the gravity of the situation, she initiated a heartfelt conversation one evening.

"Dede, I understand things take time, but we need to plan for the future. We can't put our lives on hold indefinitely." she implored.

His reply was familiarly nonchalant: *"I hear you, Amarachi. There is no need to stress. Things will work out."* He went back to his phone, chatting and laughing.

Amarachi, grappling for the right words, eventually said, *"I need you to pursue opportunities actively, not just wait for them to come* to you. *"Our future depends on it,"* she said, *grabbing the phone from him in frustration and smashing it on the floor.*

The tension in the room quickly intensified after Amarachi's impetuous action of smashing the phone. Mr Linus, clearly furious, attacked her with strong words.

"How dare you!" he yelled, his voice filled with anger. *"What gave you the audacity to collect the phone from me and smash it?"*

Before she could speak, Mr Linus swiftly raised his hand and slapped her across the face. The impact created shockwaves throughout the room, resulting in a terrible silence.

Amarachi was shocked by the severity of his betrayal and pulled away from the room, her fingers automatically moving to her face. At first, she wanted to retaliate but felt the need to remain calm. The consequences of his actions weighed heavily on the atmosphere, overshadowing their previously affectionate relationship.

She quietly walked into the children's room, where she spent the night.

Chapter Five:
Unbottled

Amarachi had been nursing suspicions about her husband since his return from Nigeria. Initially brushing them aside, she stumbled upon confirmation one day when Mr Linus carelessly left his phone unattended in the bedroom while he stepped into the bathroom. As the phone rang, Amarachi, unaccustomed to answering Mr Linus' calls, felt compelled to investigate the caller's identity. To her surprise, she discovered that Mr Linus had labelled the contact as *"My Naija Babe."* Annoyed, Amarachi impulsively accepted the WhatsApp video call, only for the lady on the other end to swiftly terminate the call upon seeing Amarachi. This encounter emboldened Amarachi to sift through Mr Linus' phone, where she stumbled upon a series of affectionate text messages. She also discovered that some of the contacts had male names; however, the profile pictures and explicit text messages showed he used those names to hide their identities. Promptly, she forwarded some of the messages to herself.

"Who was calling me?" Mr Linus inquired as he emerged from the bathroom with a towel wrapped around his waist. Age was mercilessly and conspicuously sagging his once firm eight-pack stomach.

"How would I know? Do you know how secretive you have been with your phone since you returned from Nigeria? It's practically glued to you now, and I wouldn't be surprised if you had not accidentally forgotten to take it with you into the bathroom," Amarachi responded calmly, though she found it challenging to

conceal her frustration.

As the echoes of their conversation lingered in the room, Amarachi grappled with a mix of emotions—frustration, concern, and an unwavering determination to see their shared dreams materialize despite the challenges they faced.

Weeks turned into months, and over two and half years slipped by, marked by Mr Linus' persistent inertia towards employment. Amarachi grappled with the reality of being the sole provider in the solitude of her thoughts. The traditional expectations of a husband as the primary breadwinner clashed with the unconventional dynamics of their home. Yet, in the face of this challenge, Amarachi's resilience shone through. She embraced the notion that whatever she did was for the betterment of their home, mostly the well-being of their two children.

In a quiet monologue within her mind, Amarachi acknowledged the strain but refused to let the burden of being the breadwinner define her. She found strength in the belief that she could shoulder the responsibilities even in Mr Linus' absence from active employment. Even when her colleagues gossip about their spouses at work, Amarachi never for once tells any of them what she was going through at home. The resolve strengthened her determination to persevere, to push forward, and to ensure that the unexpected turns of life would not overshadow the dreams they once shared had taken.

A subtle shift became evident in the Linus household's quiet evenings. Mr Linus, once known for his leisurely repose, now seemed engrossed in the luminous glow of his phone screen. Amarachi noticed the change but hesitated to confront the emerging pattern and the evidence she already had, waiting for the right time.

One day, the children approached Mr Linus to give them his

phone so they could play a game on it, but they were shocked by a stern warning that cut through the air. *"Stay away from my phone. Don't ever dream of touching it!"* he admonished his words carrying an authoritative tone.

Observing this sudden change, Amarachi could not help but wonder. The phone, once a tool for connection, now held an air of secrecy, shielded by a password known only to Mr Linus. Attempts to call him on the Whatsapp messaging apps during her night shifts to supplement her day work often resulted in perpetually engaged signals, leaving Amarachi with lingering questions. There were even times he would secretly disengage from the bed in the middle of the night and quietly enter the living room to make or receive calls.

Despite her mounting curiosity, she resisted the urge to confront him. Unspoken tension simmered beneath the surface, a silent acknowledgement of the growing distance between them. The phone, now a barrier rather than a bridge, cast a shadow over the once-shared moments of their lives.

One cold evening, driving home after a tedious day's job, Amarachi pulled up by the roadside with little traffic and put a call across to Grandma. She needed that privacy to unburden her heart.

"How are you and the children?" Grandma's excited voice filtered through when the phone connected.

"They are all fine, Nnenkukwu."

"And your husband?" Without even waiting for Amarachi's response, she continued, *"The house he erected in his father's compound within a short period of time is really a sight to behold! I'm highly impressed."*

"We give thanks to God." Amarachi pretended to be happy and

then wisely changed the subject. *"I believe everybody is doing well."*

"Yes, my daughter. God will always bless you for knowing you still have a mother here. Ngozi just stepped out, but she'll soon be back."

"Nnenkukwu, there's something disturbing me that I want to discuss with you," Amarachi said slowly.

"What could it be?" Grandma's initial happy voice immediately switched to a sober and anxious one.

"I don't want you to get worried; all I need now is your advice, Nnenkukwu. Honestly speaking, I'm full."

"What happened? Just tell me. There's nothing the eyes will ever see that will make them bleed."

"Why do our men dance with their shoulders?"

Grandma hesitated and then asked, *"What has that got to do with your worries?"*

"Nnenkukwu, am I not the one who called you? I'll tell you everything, but please answer me because we learn every day."

"Well, it shows that men bear the responsibility of the home and ensure the security and comfort of the home."

"And why do women dance with their waist?"

"Women provide stability and support; in fact, if that unit is faulty, everything collapses. But why all these, Amarachi?"

"Nnenkukwu, if the shoulders are faulty, what will the waist support and stabilize?"

"What are you little girl hinting at? Don't tell me something bad has happened to your husband!" Grandma said in alarm.

"No, Nnenkukwwu, nothing bad happened to him. He's alive and perfectly strong. It is me that is ..." Amarachi's voice trailed off as she began to sob, her heart wrenching apart with the heavy load.

"My child, there's no problem in this world without a solution." Grandma consoled in a teary voice, deeply touched by Amarachi's grief. "Just pull yourself together and talk to me. There must be a way out."

"Ever since he returned from building that house, I don't know him again. He's a completely different person. In the morning, when everyone is going out to look for what to do, he sits at home idling away his life, Nnenkukwu."

"Does he go out at night?" Grandma asked with concern.

"No, he doesn't either. He actually lost his regular job about two years ago, but Nnenkukwu, is that enough reason for him to stop making an effort?" She said as if ready to fight someone.

"If that be the case, don't you think it might be depression that is affecting his drive for job hunting? Have you tried encouraging him?"

"Several times without success, Nnenkukwu." Amarachi rolled her eyes in frustration.

"But wait, Amarachi," Grandma paused and swallowed before continuing. "I hope you're not starving him?"

"He's the one starving me instead!" She pouted. "He wouldn't bring money, he wouldn't say nice words, he wouldn't pick my calls, and he wouldn't bring anything. Who's starving who? Nnenkukwu?"

She poured out all her hidden pains to Grandma, and when she finished, she was drenched in sweat despite the cold weather and the crimson sun casting a melancholy glow over the surroundings.

"Amarachi, my child, is only a patient person who laps hot soup. The reason is simple: he gently circles around it until it is all done. Nobody has ever been crowned victor for winning a fight with one's spouse. Take things easy, and don't ever think of vengeance; remember, you have children now. One who farts in retaliation always ends up defecating. My child, be a good wife and a good mother; your marriage will work for sure." With many other words of wisdom, Grandma advised and encouraged Amarachi. When she was done, she tried extracting a promise from her, *"My child, you heard all that I said, right?"*

"Nnenkukwu, I heard all that you said." Amarachi respectfully answered.

"Ezigbo nwa m!" Grandma happily said as they ended the call.

Amarachi exhaled deeply and pinched her left thumb, a habit she had developed over time whenever she faced difficulty. Then, she decided to take Ifeoma, her bosom friend, into confidence.

The moment the video call connected, Amarachi was a little disappointed when she observed from the backdrop that she was still at work and some clients were still waiting to be attended to.

"I can see you're quite busy." Amarachi grins, winking at Ifeoma.

"No, no, no, no. I have capable hands. My girls can attend to them." Having said that, she quickly gave instructions, withdrew into a private room, and shut the door behind her.

"That was smart!" Amarachi praised with a thumbs up.

"One is no longer a baby, now," Ifeoma replied. "But Amarachi, na wa oh! You're getting younger and more beautiful every day. The truth is that no one will believe you have dropped two engines, eziokwu."

"Ifeoma, leave what is written on the moto and enter the moto, biko. When situations are wrapped up in George... Anyway, there's something I want to discuss with you."

"I'm all ears. Come on, are you in a car?"

"Yes, I am. See you. You're only noticing now, but I'm not driving by the roadside." They laughed and continued the discussion.

When Amarachi finished her story, Ifeoma was quite upset; she shuffled her feet irritably like she was ready for a brawl.

"When I do to you what you did to me, there should be no tears!" She exclaimed angrily. "Don't allow anyone to bottle you up! Nobody is a fool here. Just prove your worth; after all, he's not feeding you."

When the call ended, Ifeoma was still fuming; she shut down earlier than usual and went home.

Amarachi started the car and turned on the heater. Only then did she realise that the biting cold had numb her hands. She waited for a while before driving off. On the way, her mind drifted between the two approaches, but the one from Ifeoma had a stronger appeal.

The lively atmosphere of the MCC African Restaurant in Basildon, Essex, pulsed with energy as colleagues gathered for an evening of relaxation. Accompanied by her friend Chichi, Amarachi made her way to the bar to order a drink. While perusing the drinks menu, she sensed someone's gaze upon her. Glancing over, she noticed a well-dressed man exuding confidence, his eyes fixed on her with interest. As the barman took her order, Amarachi prepared to return to Chichi when the man approached and introduced himself.

"Hi! There, young lady. I'm James," he said, extending his hand towards Amarachi.

Initially tempted to brush him off, Amarachi reciprocated the gesture, replying politely, *"I'm Amarachi."*

"Is this your first time here?" James inquired, his eyes filled with genuine curiosity.

Caught off guard but intrigued by the unexpected encounter, Amarachi responded, *"No, we come here occasionally. It's a nice place to unwind after work."*

The conversation flowed effortlessly as James shared a laugh with Amarachi and Chichi.

Soon, James' friend Obinna joined the scene, and the companionship expanded as they decided to join Amarachi and Chichi at their table. When both Amarachi and Chichi realised that Obinna was from Eastern Nigeria, they almost pushed James aside, as the evening's conversation was mostly in Igbo.

Amarachi and James engaged in lively conversation, while Chichi and Obinna were engrossed in their discussion. Amidst the chatter, Amarachi found herself genuinely enjoying James' company. The warmth of their exchange seemed to dissolve the emotional void that had settled within her.

As the evening unfolded, James and Amarachi went beyond mere small talk. Their connection deepened, and as the night neared its end, James tentatively asked for Amarachi's number, a request she met with a thoughtful smile.

Driving home, Amarachi couldn't shake the feeling of connection she shared with James. The warmth of his handshake lingered, and she caught the faint scent of his cologne as she brought her hand to her nose. His presence had injected vibrancy into her otherwise mundane routine.

Meanwhile, James cruised along in his car, his thoughts consumed by Amarachi. The glint of the ring on her left hand didn't escape his notice, prompting him to ponder the complexities of her seemingly content yet intricate life.

In the solitude of her car, Amarachi's thoughts meandered through the emotional landscape of her marriage. The laughter shared with James highlighted the void that had grown between her and Mr Linus. As she yearned to fill that void, James represented an unexpected spark that ignited a yearning for connection, understanding, and the thrill of rediscovering herself amidst the complexities of life and love.

Upon arriving home, Amarachi was embraced by the soothing familiarity of her surroundings. She discovered Mr Linus was in the living room, deeply absorbed in his phone, and involved in a discussion that fully captured his attention.

Amarachi stood next to him and attempted to have a normal conversation. *"How was your day, dear?"* she said, her voice tinged with fatigue from the day's events.

Mr Linus, preoccupied with his phone, gave a vague answer, hardly looking up from the screen. *"The usual,"* he said, splitting his focus between the phone discussion and Amarachi standing next to him.

When she discovered Mr Linus was deeply absorbed in his phone, she gently excused herself and went to the bedroom. As she lay down on the bed, she could still hear Mr Linus' faint conversation echoing in her ears.

Amarachi was lost in thoughts about her meeting with James; she recalled fragments of her discussion with James, each recollection sparking a surge of emotions; her mind wandered in the silent chamber, repeating the evening's events like scenes from a movie. Unbeknownst to her, sleep gradually crept upon her, wrapping her in its gentle embrace. The rhythmic sound of her breathing filled the room, the only indication of her peaceful slumber. As the night wore on, Amarachi remained oblivious to the passage of time, her mind still adrift in a sea of contemplation and introspection.

With the morning sun streaming through her window the following morning, her phone buzzed at exactly 10:13am, signalling a text message. When she picked up her phone, she realised the text was from a number not on her contact.

"Good morning, Amarachi; how was your night? This is James. Do you still remember me?"

Amarachi smiled as she read the message. *"Good morning, James! Of course, I remember you,"* she replied, her fingers dancing across the screen. *"My night was peaceful, thank you. How about yours?"*

As she waited for his response, Amarachi could not help but feel a flutter of excitement at the prospect of continuing their conversation from the previous evening. The warmth of their connection lingered in her thoughts, filling her with anticipation for what the day might bring.

They engaged in a virtual dance of words, sharing bits of their lives and the ties that bound them. Each message felt like adding to a painting of shared experiences and silent agreement.

James's response to Amarachi's revelation about her marriage echoed through her thoughts. *"I appreciate your honesty and want to assure you that I fully respect the sanctity of marriage,"* he affirmed. His words carried a weight that made her ponder the complexities of connections, responsibilities, and the human need for companionship.

"I am happily married myself," James responded. *But can we remain friends?"* James asked in his text.

"Hmm, it depends on the type of friendship," she replied cautiously, testing the waters. To her surprise, James responded with a thoughtful explanation of his beliefs. He saw connections and friendships as integral to human experience, capable of bringing joy, support, and personal growth.

Intrigued by the depth of their conversation, Amarachi clarified her boundaries, making it clear that she wasn't open to any form of intimacy. James, in turn, respected her stance, assuring her of his commitment to a genuine, casual friendship.

As the day progressed, Amarachi discovered solace in the written exchanges with James. Their virtual dialogues became a sanctuary, providing intellectual engagement and a sense of understanding she craved in her daily life. Their messages flowed effortlessly each day, with James making it a routine to send morning greetings, weaving a tapestry of connection that reached beyond their screens. Amid her day-to-day responsibilities, Amarachi's thoughts frequently drifted towards her exchanges with James. The text messages, the moments of joy they shared and the companionship that blossomed from their chatting all provided a welcomed escape from the tensions at home. The allure of their growing friendship became a beacon of light in the shadows that lurked in her domestic landscape.

Within days, Amarachi and James established the parameters of their friendship and decided on the best times for their exchanges. As they wished each other a joyful day, the unspoken question lingered in Amarachi's mind – *what if this connection, forged through words, could evolve into something more daring?* The prospect of exploring this uncharted territory held a sense of excitement and uncertainty for both Amarachi and James, adding a layer of complexity to her unfolding story.

Chapter Six:
The Trigger Escapades

After a month of digital intimacy, James felt an overwhelming need to transcend the confines of their virtual connection.

"Good morning, my dearest Amarachi. I hope this message brightens your day as much as your presence lights up mine," James texted with affection.

"Good morning, James. Your messages never fail to bring a smile to my face," Amarachi replied, her heart warmed by his words.

As days melted into weeks, James and Amarachi's clandestine bond deepened. Their virtual exchanges wove intricate threads, blurring the boundaries between friendship and longing. James, the master of expressive messages, continued to send his morning greetings, each word a stroke on the canvas of their hidden relationship.

"After two months of shared thoughts and emotions, Amarachi, I feel compelled to see you and hear your voice's melody in person. What do you say? Can we meet?" James proposed in his message to Amarachi.

"James, I... I'm not sure. Meeting face-to-face feels like crossing a line, doesn't it?" she replied, torn by conflicting emotions.

"Perhaps, but haven't our words already crossed so many lines? The meeting is just another step in unravelling the mysteries we've woven." he reasoned.

Despite her initial hesitation, Amarachi found comfort in James' words. Their hearts resonated with the shared understanding of the complexities that entwined them in a delicate web of secrets.

In time, they arranged to meet at the same restaurant that had become the backdrop of their clandestine connection. The air crackled with anticipation as they faced each other, navigating the unspoken tension that enveloped them.

When it was time to part ways in the dimly lit car park, their eyes locked in a charged gaze. The stillness of the night resonated with the magnitude of their penetrating gazes. The moment exuded an unmistakable sense of forbidden desire, tantalisingly close yet concealed by the unpredictability of one's capacity to restrain oneself. They were compelled, apparently, by an imperceptible force to succumb to the undeniable magnetism between them, and they engaged in a fervent kiss despite the boundaries they had earlier set.

The unexpected intimacy left Amarachi startled. Swiftly, she detached herself and hurried to her car, leaving James standing alone, grappling with the consequences of their impulsive actions. The echoes of their unspoken desires lingered in the night, and Amarachi's abrupt departure cast a shadow over the growing connection.

In the following week, Amarachi's silence became a heavy weight for James. He wondered about the impact of their shared moment and blamed himself for succumbing to the magnetic pull of the atmosphere. Despite the internal turmoil, he recognized that resisting the allure of that charged moment might have been an exercise in futility.

Amarachi's reluctance to respond to James' messages created an unsettling void, and self-blame weighed heavily on him. However, he reasoned that taking action in such a charged atmosphere was an inevitable consequence. The delicate dance of their secret affair took an unexpected turn.

James could not stop thinking about his actions. *"What have I done? Did I push too far?" With that type of charged atmosphere, resisting the pull felt impossible. I can't blame myself for succumbing to the tension"*. He consoled himself.

After two weeks of sending messages and no response from Amarachi, James resolved within himself to give her space.

Another week passed in silence, leaving James consumed by self-blame. He was on the verge of logging out of his work computer one evening when a text message popped up on his phone. Initially, he was tempted to ignore it until he got home, but something urged him to read it. It was a message from Amarachi!

"Hi James, how have you been? Can we meet this Friday evening at 7 pm at the reception of De Facto on 22 Belgrave Street, SE2 3AA?"

As James absorbed the message, a mix of relief and caution washed over him. Though his initial impulse was to ignore it, he found himself replying in the affirmative. As he drives home, he mulled over Amarachi's request to meet at a different location.

As they sat facing each other, apologies lingered in the air. In an attempt to douse the tension, James started, *"Amarachi, I've been wrestling with that night in the car park. I didn't mean to make you uncomfortable. It was impulsive, and I regret if it crossed any boundaries."*

Amarachi, fidgeting with her Audi Q3 car key, responded, *"James, it's not just you. I've been wrestling, too, with emotions I* never thought I'd feel. That kiss caught me off guard. I left because I didn't know how to handle it."

"I know you must be confused about my decision not to respond to your messages since we parted ways at that car park three weeks ago," she began.

James was about to offer a further apology when Amarachi interjected, "I should be the one apologizing, James. I left abruptly because I felt emotionally overwhelmed."

Their eyes met, and in that shared gaze, a silent understanding passed between them. James, sensing her vulnerability, replied, "I never meant to push you into something you weren't ready for. I value what we have, and I respect your boundaries."

Amarachi, looking down at her plate, admitted, "It's not that I'm not ready, James. It's that I'm terrified of the consequences. We're both married, and the world would never understand."

As the night progressed, Amarachi suggested to James that he shouldn't rush to leave, revealing that she had already booked a room at the guest house for them to spend the night.

"Spend the night?" James said, taken aback.

"Yes, I've already informed my husband that I'll be working tonight. And you can call your wife to let her know you won't be home early," Amarachi reassured him.

James hesitated, contemplating what he would tell his wife. Eventually, he made the call to inform her that he would be returning home late, explaining that he was out with Obinor for the evening.

Their conversation, laden with unspoken desires and fears, navigated the uncharted territory of their forbidden connection. As they sipped their drinks, the atmosphere shifted from apology to curiosity. James, with a half-smile, asked, *"What is it that drew you to me, Amarachi? What are you seeking in this connection?"*

Amarachi, tracing the rim of her glass with her fingertip, replied, *"It's not about seeking something new, James. It's about finding what's missing. In the complexity of our lives, there's an emotional void that we stumbled upon. And for a moment, that void felt less daunting."*

Their conversation delved into the intricacies of their marriages, the unspoken desires, and the unmet needs that brought them to this clandestine rendezvous. As the evening unfolded, they shared more than just stolen glances; they shared pieces of their lives that had long been hidden.

Amarachi and James indulged in a few drinks at the guest house bar. The atmosphere grew more intimate with each passing moment, as the dim lighting and soft music created a seductive atmosphere.

As they finished their drinks, Amarachi, with a subtle glint in her eyes, suggested, *"Shall we head to our room?"*

James hesitated, his internal struggle evident. *"Are you sure about this?"* he questioned, uncertainty clouding his expression.

Amarachi, undeterred, took his hand, leading him towards the room. The anticipation in the air was palpable as they entered the space where the lines between desire and restraint began to blur.

Inside the room, the intensity of the moment hung in the air. Their eyes locked, and as James hesitated, their magnetic pull intensified. Suddenly, the world outside ceased to exist, and they found themselves entwined in a passionate embrace.

James, wrestling with the internal conflict between desire and morality, gently pulled back from the intensity of their shared moment. *"Amarachi, we can't keep going down this path. It's wrong,"* he uttered, his voice laced with both regret and conviction.

Amarachi, her eyes reflecting a mix of emotions, nodded reluctantly. *"I know, James. It's just... It's hard to resist what we feel for each other,"* she admitted, her voice whispering in the dimly lit room.

James paused as his determination weakened in response to their mutual desire. *"I know,"* he said, his voice filled with anguish. *"I understand the complications, Amarachi. I've never been in a situation like this before. It's as new and confusing for me as it is for you."*

As they navigated the delicate conversation, James hesitated, torn between the responsibilities that anchored him and the magnetic force drawing him closer to Amarachi. A shared silence lingered, laden with unspoken desires.

In a moment fraught with palpable tension, James hesitated once more, his eyes ensnared by Amarachi's magnetic gaze. The gravitational pull between them intensified, compelling them to yield to the irresistible allure. In an unspoken accord, they surrendered to the overwhelming desire, their lips meeting in a fervent kiss that ignited the very air around them.

Within the confines of the room, their shared longing seemed to pulse with an energy all its own. As inhibitions dissolved, the soft strains of Celine Dion's "My Heart Will Go On" seeping in from the nearby bar only served to heighten the atmosphere.

In that intimate space, their union transcended mere physicality, delving into realms of profound connection and ecstasy. Each touch, each whispered breath, carried them to heights previously unexplored, leaving them both gasping for air, their souls intertwined in a euphoria that surpassed any previous encounter.

Barely less than one week after their first romantic encounter, the decision to meet again lingered in the air, and they made the guest's house their regular place of meeting. Amarachi's mind echoed with the reverberations of their conversation. The intricacies of their connection had deepened, and the unspoken boundaries blurred further. In the silent moments between meetings, Amarachi and James grappled with the consequences of a connection that defied societal norms.

Two weeks after their last encounter, Amarachi and James once again found solace in each other's arms. Their connection evolved into a dance of passion that defied the boundaries of their respective lives. The hushed whispers of endearments and the entwining of fingers spoke of a shared intimacy that momentarily eclipsed the complexities of their situations.

Amidst shared laughter and stolen kisses, Amarachi could not help but marvel at the energy James brought to their clandestine encounter. *"James,"* she teased, *"where on earth do you get this boundless energy from?"*

He chuckled, the warmth of their connection evident in his eyes. *"Maybe it's the joy of being with you, Amarachi. You bring a lightness to my world that I hadn't known before."*

"But are you not afraid of getting pregnant"? James asked during one of their encounters.

"Don't be silly, James", she teased. *"I am on family planning."*

Their conversation, free from guilt and inhibition, unfolded like a love story written in stolen moments. Amarachi, basking in the newfound hope and love that James seemed to ignite within her, shared, *"You make me feel alive, James. In these moments, I've found a version of myself that I had forgotten existed."*

The irony of her situation didn't escape her. While her marriage with Mr Linus languished in a state of lethargy, her connection with James rekindled a flame within her. Amarachi could not find it in herself to feel guilty, for she saw this affair as a lifeline rather than a transgression.

Reflecting on her marital struggles, Amarachi recalled the times she had attempted to help Mr Linus find work, only to face rejection. She explained to James, *"I've tried, James. I've searched for job opportunities, and I have paid for different trainings that could land him a job, but he never bothers to complete any; it's like he doesn't want to put in the effort. Laziness has taken over, and I find myself becoming the sole provider."* *"It's like he married me to come and work to sustain the family."* She concluded as she became emotional.

Their conversation shifted to the unsettling discovery Amarachi made about Mr Linus' secretive actions. With a hint of frustration, she shared, *"And the other day, I saw those text messages on his phone. Sending money to girls in Nigeria. My hard-earned money, James. It's as if he's taking advantage of my trust and my resources."*

James listened empathetically, understanding the tangled threads of her emotions. *"Amarachi, you deserve better. You deserve to be appreciated for all your efforts." However, I wouldn't want you to take any step that could destabilise the children*". He concluded.

As the dawn approached, Amarachi and James lingered in the afterglow of their shared passion. In the soft moments that followed, Amarachi could not help but express, *"I've never felt so free, James. Thank you for being my escape."*

Their final conversation echoed promises of more stolen moments, more shared laughter, and the acknowledgement that their connection, though born out of forbidden circumstances, was becoming an undeniable force in both their lives. Whenever they parted ways, the complexities of their situations lingered, but in the realm of their secret love affair, Amarachi and James found a refuge that momentarily shielded them from the realities waiting beyond the walls of the guest house.

The morning light filtered through the curtains, casting a gentle glow on the aftermath of their clandestine encounter. James and Amarachi lay entwined, their fingers tracing patterns on bare skin, as if reluctant to let go of the stolen moments they'd shared. The room, once a sanctuary for their secret passion, now bore witness to the delicate dance between desire and reality.

In the weeks that followed, the magnetic pull between Amarachi and James drew them back to the familiar confines of the guest house, where they sought solace in each other's arms. Despite the lingering shadows of guilt and uncertainty, their desire for one another eclipsed all else, leading them back to the haven where their forbidden love could flourish away from prying eyes.

"James, these moments with you... they feel like a breath of fresh air amidst everything else," Amarachi murmured in contentment, her eyes reflecting contemplation as she spoke softly.

James fixed his gaze on her and smiled with a tenderness that bespoke a connection deeper than the physical.

"Amarachi, I don't know where this path will take us, but I know that being with you feels right. Let's cherish what we have, even if it exists in the shadows."

As they dressed and prepared to leave the guest house, the weight of reality pressed upon them. Amarachi hesitated, her mind wrestling with the complexities of her dual life. *"James, I've never done anything like this before. It's exhilarating, but a part of me is scared."*

He reached for her hand, offering reassurance. *"Amarachi, we're navigating uncharted waters together. It's natural to feel a mix of emotions. What matters is that we're honest with each other and ourselves."*

Their conversation continued outside the guest house, the crisp morning air a stark contrast to the warmth they'd shared just moments ago. *"I know I have responsibilities at home,"* Amarachi admitted, her gaze fixed on the ground. *"But being with you makes me forget all my worries."*

James nodded in understanding. *"Amarachi, we can't change our circumstances overnight. What we can do is find solace in each other and enjoy the moments we steal away. Life is too short to deny ourselves happiness."*

As they parted ways, James whispered, *"Until next time, Amarachi,"* and the unspoken understanding between them lingered in the air. The drive back to their respective abode was marked by a contemplative silence.

Days turned into weeks, and their secret liaison continued – a delicate balance between the forbidden and the liberating. Text messages became lifelines, each word a testament to the connection they shared. Conversations ranged from the mundane to the profound, threading through the intricacies of their lives and the undeniable attraction that bound them together.

Their stolen moments continued, the bond between them growing stronger with each encounter. In the intimate exchanges that followed, Amarachi and James explored the intricacies of their desires, finding in each other a sanctuary that momentarily shielded them from the complexities beyond the walls of the guest house.

As Amarachi navigated through the days that followed, she couldn't shake the contrast of her extramarital affair against the backdrop of her marital turmoil. The emotional conflicts brewed within her, spinning like a tempest threatening to disrupt the delicate balance she had crafted.

"When was the last time I felt such passion, such desire? The thrill of James' touch lingers, and I find solace in moments stolen from the chaos of my life. Yet, the warning he gave resonates, a constant reminder of the precarious line I tread."

Amarachi questioned herself in the quietude of her thoughts, grappling with the choices she had made. The days blurred into nights, each one a silent battleground between the satisfaction of her secret joy and the awareness of the moral tightrope she walked.

"What am I doing? This secrecy, this hidden joy—I never imagined my life would take such a turn."

The corridors of her conscience echoed with conflicting voices as she sought solace in the arms of her extramarital connection. The emotional tempest within her intensified, leading to conversations with Mr Linus that seemed more like orchestrated performances than genuine exchanges.

"Is everything okay, Amarachi?" he queried, his concern genuine yet met with vague responses that concealed the true turmoil within her.

"I'm just tired and exhausted from dealing with work and home," she offered, concealing the deeper complexities that brewed beneath

the surface.

"You know I've been looking for work," Mr Linus retorted, a hint of frustration tainting his words.

"I know, but no one gets a job the way you are going about it. This is almost three years of your job-hunting," Amarachi replied.

The impact of Amarachi's choices extended beyond the realm of her inner turmoil, casting shadows over her family dynamics, without knowing that the observant eyes of her children noted the changes in their once vibrant home.

One afternoon, while playing with the children in the room, Amarachi suddenly drifted off to sleep. In her drowsy state, she overheard a conversation between her two sons, who were engrossed in playing with their roadblocks.

"Mom seems happier lately," remarked Chinonso, the younger child.

"But why is Dad always at home and on the phone? He only takes us to school, brings us back home, and occasionally to the park, while Mom is the one out there making money for the house," observed Chibuzor.

The room held a hushed atmosphere as the children grappled with the shifting dynamics they sensed within their family, their innocent questions hanging in the air like unspoken reflections of the changes that had silently crept into their lives.

As Amarachi dozed off, her sons' words echoed in her subconscious. The weight of their observations lingered, prompting her to reflect on the shifting dynamics of their household. Despite her exhaustion, she couldn't shake off the concern that had been silently brewing within her. The realisation that her children were attuned to the changes in their family dynamic stirred a mix of emotions within her, leaving her grappling with the complexities of their situation.

Amarachi was caught between the echoes of guilt and the undeniable allure of James' companionship in the backdrop of their secret love affair. The complexities of their situations, their marriages, and the societal norms they defied were woven into the fabric of their clandestine connection, creating a delicate web of secrets that threatened to unravel with each stolen moment.

As Amarachi and James journeyed through their complex lives, they grappled with balancing their desires and responsibilities. Their secret affair offered comfort but also posed risks, tempting them with forbidden thrills while testing the stability of their futures.

Chapter Seven:
AMARACHI'S REFLECTIONS

Amarachi sought comfort in her preferred corner of the room, illuminated by the soft glow of the descending sun. The serene atmosphere offered a safe setting for profound reflections. Amarachi contemplated the complexities of her life and marriage as a gentle breeze flowed through the open window, carrying the fragrance of blooming flowers. Each passing moment in this tranquil environment irresistibly urged her to explore the intricacies of her existence and unravel the complexities that had accumulated over time.

As she retraced her experiences' intricate trajectory, a zealous determination emanated from her eyes, symbolising resolve. She analysed the complex strands that compose her life's tapestry, acknowledging every discreet element that led to this point.

She stood up, took a cup of water and reached for her diary. "My expedition has been characterised by a series of haphazard choices that led me into unexplored domains."

As Amarachi let her thoughts run freely in the quiet room, where only the sound of rustling leaves could be heard, her monologue emerged, devoid of remorse but filled with understanding and acceptance, resonating deeply within her. She yawned, stretched and gazed upwards.

"These pages record my journey, filled with unexpected turns and discoveries. The strength lies in recognising shadows and understanding the complexities of love and desire. I am characterised by my ability to confront mistakes rather than being defined by them."

Once an open notebook packed with her thoughts, confessions, and raw feelings, written during the quiet night hours, she now marvelled at the evolution of her own story. The written phrases preserved the happiness, enlightenment, and unexpressed desires of her innermost being.

" These pages record my journey, filled with unexpected turns and discoveries. The strength lies in recognising shadows and comprehending the intricacies of love and desire. I am characterised by my ability to confront mistakes rather than being defined by them," she repeated silently, moving only her lips.

In silence, Amarachi's thoughts shifted towards the broader concepts of love, commitment, and the essence of marriage.

"What is marriage?" she pondered aloud, and the question weighed heavily on her mind like a profound enigma. Is it merely a contract for procreation, a societal structure to ensure the continuity of lineage? Or does it encompass something deeper, something intangible yet essential?"

The sound of a metallic object falling in the children's room momentarily disrupted her flow of thought as she hurried to check on the boys. It was the empty can of the drink that the boys had taken before sleeping that was displaced by their falling blanket. She covered them properly with the blanket, threw the can into the trash bin, and returned to her sanctuary. On her way back, she could hear Linus' peaceful snore in the living room.

"Marriage transcends mere physical proximity; it is a union of intellects, emotions, and spirits. It surpasses the basic function of procreation and societal conventions," she mused. As she reflected on her initial reluctance to marry Linus, a question reverberated through her mind: "Is marriage an ultimate objective or merely a pathway to attain one?" She picked up her pen and wrote:

"Family pressure and societal expectations forced me into a commitment for which I was unprepared."

"Linus, a chapter in my life. His presence, once the focal point of my world, is now a distant element in the vast expanse of my narrative. His vision of marriage was rooted in duty and tradition. His top priority was establishing a family, often at the expense of being present to support and encourage me in my studies and career." Her face contorted into a masque of fleshy grimace. "Marriage," she continued, "is more than shared goals and dreams. It requires mutual understanding, support, and the willingness to grow together. When partners drift apart in their aspirations, the very foundation of their union is tested."

Amarachi reflected on the disparity in their goals, and her nostrils quivered.

"I realised that Linus' aspiration to build a house in the village, motivated by cultural norms, ran counter to my own aspiration to advance professionally in the United Kingdom, which I perceived as a means to secure a stable position and foster a sense of community in our adopted country. "Cultural factors influenced Linus' priorities," He squandered his hard-earned redundancy payment on a symbol of his heritage back home while I longed for integration and advancement."

Linus' waning interest in intimacy shortly after the arrival of their second child frequently made her feel ignored. This divergence in goals strained their relationship, creating a chasm that grew wider with time.

She pondered the potential influence of the significant age difference on Linus' diminishing sexual drive: "Could our physical and emotional estrangement have their origins in this disparity?" She inquired voicelessly, tightening her lips. The biological reflection of their marital union prompted her to question whether her union with Linus had ever truly satisfied her ambitions and desires. "Did my matrimonial union with Linus truly satisfy my desires, or was it merely a duty-driven decision?"

In this sacred space, she found refuge in self-discovery. The consequences of her actions surfaced from the depths of memory like phantoms. She confronted them directly, recognising their influence on her life.

"Consequences are the reverberations of our decisions." "I do not avoid them. I learn, adapt, and grow stronger. "By enduring arduous circumstances, I cultivated fortitude, thereby revealing the essence of my being." She paused and looked through the window.

After meticulously examining the intricate progression of her experiences, analysing the multifaceted interconnections that shaped the tapestry of her life, and recognising each nuanced component that had contributed to her present state of being, she determined that her journey was turbulent, marked by decisions that had propelled her into uncharted territories. As she immersed herself in the room's silence, interrupted only by the rustling of leaves, her internal dialogue emerged, lacking any sense of regret but brimming with understanding and acceptance.

"My personal account," she scribbled on, "once a collection of my reflections, admissions, and unfiltered sentiments transcribed during the nocturnal hours, now fills me with admiration for its development. The written expressions have encapsulated the fundamental nature of my most profound emotions, evoking sentiments of delight, comprehension, and latent desires." These pages chronicle my odyssey, replete with unexpected detours and revelations. "Understanding the complexities of longing and affection, as well as perceiving darkness, are the keys to achieving power. Merely confronting my mistakes distinguishes me instead of permitting them to define me."

The sharp call of an owl in the distance startled her a little, bringing back memories of her childhood. She hissed, shook her head vigorously, and continued writing. "Life is an unforeseen tapestry interwoven with threads of joy and sorrow. Every decision and deviation contributes to the intricate formation. I chose a less conventional path, fully embracing the complex elements that influenced my sense of self. Remorse impedes advancement; hence, I acknowledge their impact on my existence and confront them head-on."

Amarachi's attention turned to James, and her face beamed with a delightful smile. A man sixteen years younger than Linus, James had rejuvenated her life and captured her attention.

"James," she whispered inadvertently, "demonstrated attentiveness, allocated time for me, and consistently sent endearing messages on a daily basis." Her smile broadened as she scanned through these messages on her phone. "He rekindled my sense of femininity and bestowed the affection and attention that Linus had ceased to provide, resulting in the covert nature of our relationship."

"The times they spent together were a clear juxtaposition to Linus' inclination to chat on his phone rather than dedicate time and attention to her. 'Did I feel love, or was it lust?' she wondered.

"Although the extramarital relationship with James offered solace from my marital concerns, it remained obscured by the stigma of social criticism. 'Our time together brought me solace, yet our love defied conventions, a bond we could never openly acknowledge without fear of condemnation.'"

In public, such a truth would be met with scorn and disbelief."

"As she delved deeper into her reflections, she questioned the essence of her bond with James. 'Could it stem from my unmet needs and desires, or was it a genuine emotional bond?' Through his embrace, I found parts of myself that had long been dormant, yet the relationship was fundamentally transient, existing only in the shadows of our lives." She caught a glimpse of her image in the wall mirror and marvelled at her transformation.

"Before encountering James, I frequently sought comfort in my pillows, experiencing a profound sense of emptiness," she reminisced. James filled the emptiness, providing her with a sense of recognition and worth. Although she recognised the immorality of engaging in extramarital affairs, she experienced no remorse. "I required relief from the financial strain of being the breadwinner of our household while living with a man who appeared apathetic towards my needs and labour to ensure our home did not crumble." However, to whom can I entrust such a sensitive matter that is considered socially unacceptable?

"She contemplated the potential consequences of never crossing paths with James. 'Would I have persisted in experiencing a sense of dissatisfaction and isolation?' she pondered. The affair, although morally intricate, brought attention to the emotional and physical requirements that her marriage did not fulfil. She asked, 'Does marriage or culture exempt us from discussing sex and intimacy in marriage?' acknowledging that her own relationship often overlooked such conversations.

Amarachi reminisced about stolen evenings when she and James shared intimate moments filled with vulnerability and love, transcending time constraints. 'In peaceful moments, his words linger in the air like a sweet tune,' she recalled. 'Your grin,' he said, 'brightens even the darkest corners of my universe." His praise was not mere flattery but a reflection of a profound connection that went beyond the ordinary. His touch evoked a myriad of feelings that enriched our mutual desires.'

As she recalled the specifics of their encounters, the moon illuminated Amarachi's face. Every secret kiss and murmured confession became a cherished treasure stored deep within her heart. 'Our forbidden and passionate love grew in the dimly lit gardens of our secret encounters,' she pondered. 'The surreptitious gaze, brimming with implicit commitments, carried the weight of a realm exclusively reserved for us.' At that time, I was not carrying out the duties of a wife or a mother but instead delving into the intricacies of my own desires."

"James was the originator of experiences that exceeded the boundaries imposed by societal norms. Their meetings served not only as a means of being physically close to each other but also as a display of the tenacity of the human heart and a joyful acknowledgement of the emotional sanctuary they created for one another. 'In James' embrace, I felt valued, cherished and loved. I discovered dormant facets of my being that had remained inactive for an extended period,' she pondered. 'Our covert connection was highly evident because of the intricate entanglement of our lives.' Love exhibits itself in various forms, thriving without consideration for societal limitations.".

"As the night grew darker, Amarachi's contemplations shifted towards the wider concepts of Westernisation, femininity, and the enigmas surrounding marriage. 'The process of Westernisation offered the prospect of freedom and prospects,' she pondered; 'however, it also introduced intricacies that posed a challenge to my conventional principles.' The conflict between her cultural heritage and her unfamiliar environment resulted in a pervasive tension that affected her marriage and her personal sense of self.

"Marriage," she pondered, "is more than a mere legal agreement or a societal duty. This is a psychological odyssey, a quest to delve into our most profound longings and anxieties." She often felt burdened by the implicit societal expectations placed on women. "We are required to maintain a harmonious blend of traditional values and contemporary practices while simultaneously fulfilling the roles of dutiful daughters, devoted wives, caring mothers, and accomplished professionals." However, can we fulfil all these responsibilities without compromising our identity?"

"Amarachi's experiences enlightened her to the fact that marriage is a complex and diverse institution influenced by cultural, emotional, and psychological factors. 'The implicit aspect of Westernisation has revealed to me that the quest for individual satisfaction frequently entails sacrificing conventional principles.' However, this does not establish one path as superior to the other. It merely underscores the intricacy of our existence.

The sun's last rays illuminated the room, casting amber and gold hues. During periods of introspection, Amarachi felt a new inner power—a resilient spark that could not be extinguished.

As the night deepened, Amarachi's reflections settled into a serene acceptance of her past choices and their implications. "This room, my sanctuary, is free from judgment,' she thought. 'Here, I untangle the threads to create a more intricate and detailed tapestry. I am prepared to write the next chapter of my life, celebrating new beginnings."

Amarachi embraced the lessons of her past in this reverent space of introspection, devoid of criticism. "Every experience, whether filled with happiness or suffering, adds to the intricate fabric of my being," she concluded. As she prepared to write the next chapter of her life, she found peace in acknowledging her personal journey, ready to face the future with newly acquired wisdom and resilience.

Amarachi's contemplation of her uncertain future became more profound as the night progressed. Enveloped in darkness, the room appeared to assimilate her thoughts, compelling her to contemplate her subsequent course of action. She experienced a sense of conflict and indecision as she considered different options, each presenting its own difficulties and unknown outcomes.

At certain moments, the idea of divorcing Linus appeared attractive. "Is it possible for me to discover happiness and fulfilment outside the limitations of a marriage that no longer benefits me?" she pondered. The prospect of autonomy—establishing a fresh existence liberated from the emotional weight of an unsatisfying partnership—was alluring. However, the repercussions of making such a choice weighed heavily on her thoughts, and she was brimming with apprehension about societal scrutiny and the effect on her children.

An alternative option was to reunite with Linus. "Is it possible to rediscover the path to one another and reignite the affection that previously united us?" she pondered. The possibility of repairing their broken relationship, resolving their disagreements, and re-establishing the closeness they had lost offered a ray of hope. However, she harboured doubts that they could surmount the entrenched problems that had caused their separation.

"What would be the consequences of disclosing my extramarital affairs to Linus? Would it be morally right to 'reconcile' and still conceal such amorous affairs from him?"

Resisting the urge to end her affair with James was a difficult challenge for her. "James evokes a sense of vitality and desirability within me; he brought back my youthfulness," she reflected. The covert nature of their affair introduced a sense of exhilaration, providing a break from the monotony of her everyday existence. However, can a relationship founded on concealment and dishonesty ever offer the stability and satisfaction she genuinely desires?

Despite its challenging nature, terminating her romantic involvement with James was a viable option that she had to contemplate. "Can I conclude this chapter of my life and discover the fortitude to depart from a love that challenged societal norms?" she contemplated. The concept of relinquishing James and reverting to a life characterised by duty and responsibility engendered a profound feeling of grief within her. However, it also provided an opportunity for her to reorient her life according to her principles and pursue satisfaction in a manner that respected her obligations.

The ambiguity of her future burdened Amarachi as she contemplated these potential outcomes. The room, currently enveloped in the tranquillity of the night, seemed to echo her internal conflict. The answers remained elusive, much like the shadows that flickered on the walls, leaving her journey without a definite conclusion and brimming with potential outcomes.

Amarachi shut her eyes, embracing the serenity of self-consciousness and the potential of fresh starts. She felt a sense of relief and determination as she got ready to embrace the unpredictable journey of her life.

ADDITIONAL RESOURCES

If you resonate with Amarachi's story or find yourself in a similar situation, know that you are not alone. Many women share her experiences of balancing family responsibilities, career ambitions, and personal dreams.

At GAFIN Charitable Foundation, we understand these challenges and offer tailored support and resources. Our charitable organisation provides services to help you navigate these difficulties.

How to Reach Out:

Visit our dedicated page at

Website: www.gafincharitablefoundation.org/Amarachi

Email: support@gafincharitablefoundation.org

for more information on how we can assist you. You'll find detailed information about our services and how to contact our support team there.

Remember, seeking help is a sign of strength. We're here to support you every step of the way, providing the resources and care you need to navigate your challenges and build a brighter future. You are not alone; together, we can create a path to healing and empowerment.

www.ingramcontent.com/pod-product-compliance
Lightning Source LLC
LaVergne TN
LVHW050029080526
838202LV00070B/6971